Next Thing to Strangers

Next Thing to Strangers

SHERI COOPER SINYKIN

LOTHROP, LEE & SHEPARD BOOKS
NEW YORK

ACKNOWLEDGEMENTS

Special thanks to Nikki Behrens, for planting the seed; to Linda McFerren, my sons' teacher and my one-woman rooting section; to Linda Pieper Skaaland and Sherie Sondel, for their friendship and advice; and to my editor, Judit Z. Bodnar, for helping me shape my vision.

 Inquiries should be addressed to Lothrop, Lee & Shepard Books, a division of William Morrow & Company, Inc., 1350 Avenue of the Americas, New York, New York 10019. Printed in the United States of America

First Edition 1 2 3 4 5 6 7 8 9 10

Library of Congress Cataloging in Publication Data

Sinykin, Sheri Cooper.

Next thing to strangers / by Sheri Cooper Sinykin. p. cm. Summary: While visiting their grandparents at a trailer park in Arizona, a diabetic boy and an overweight girl become friends and learn a lesson about self-acceptance. ISBN 0-688-10694-3 [1. Grandparents—Fiction. 2. Diabetes—Fiction. 3. Weight control—Fiction. 4. Friendship—Fiction.] I. Title.

PZ7.S6194Ne 1991 [Fic]—dc20 90-25991 CIP AC

TO MUTTI AND DAD—
who believed in me long before
In Shining Amor,
and still do.

Next Thing to Strangers

Chapter 1

As the jet dipped between two red mountain chains outside of Phoenix, Cass McFerren cinched her seat belt tighter. Her turkey-and-croissant snack rolled over in her stomach with the swift descent, and her fingers dug into the armrests. What was she more afraid of—airplane landings or her grandparents not being there, waiting at the gate? She had to get a grip on herself and stop imagining the worst. Yes, the plane would land safely, and *of course* they'd be there. They'd sent her the ticket, hadn't they?

Cass chided herself, and tried to conjure up some image of her father's parents. But her clearest memory was courtesy of Polaroid, and there was no way to tell how they'd aged since the snapshot had been taken. In all the years since Daddy's death, couldn't they at least have written or called? Mom's explanation was simple and always the same: "They went out of our lives when he did." But somehow that wasn't enough. Not for Cass, anyhow.

A familiar wave of resentment washed aside her fears. Some grandparents they were. No wonder she didn't trust them to show up. The weird thing was Mom insisting that Cass spend Christmas with them in the first place. No doubt Mom had big plans of her own—skiing with her latest jock-boyfriend from the university, or maybe driving up to Minneapolis to see that gymnast-guy who'd graduated last June. The McFerrens' invitation to Cass had probably been too convenient for her to question, let alone to turn down. Now *that* was a comforting thought—being shunted aside at Christmas by your own mother. At least her grandparents wanted her.

But why now? she wondered. Why now, after all these years?

Despite her anger, a squirmy excitement worked its way up from the pit of her stomach. Her long-imagined grandparents had finally sent for her; she'd always dreamed they would. Better late than never, right? Forgive and forget, that's what she had to do. At least they were rescuing her from another boring winter vacation in Iowa City.

As the plane touched down, she pulled a tiny mirror from her purse. It was just the right size for checking her hair, which (mercifully) always cooperated, and for glossing her lips, the only feature she could actually call thin. What I can't see in that mirror, she thought, is beyond my control anyway, so why worry?

The other passengers hustled into the aisle, laden with tote bags, tennis racquets, and shopping bags brimming with wrapped Christmas gifts. Cass gathered her purse and nylon duffel bag, then made a couple of vain attempts at snagging her coat from the overhead bin. At last she climbed onto the seat to rescue her down parka.

"You won't be a-needing that here," the man behind her said. He was dressed in white slacks, a yellow polo shirt, and a deep tan.

Cass eyed her hiking boots, blue jeans, and black University of Iowa sweatshirt ruefully. "Guess not," she mumbled. Her grandparents were going to think she was some kind of idiot, wearing Yukon clothes to the Valley of the Sun.

Swept along by the other passengers, Cass shuffled forward, out of the cabin, and into the narrow passageway leading to the terminal. She surveyed the sea of waiting faces, hoping to somehow recognize Ed and Leah McFerren. The last time Cass had seen them was eleven years before, when she was three. But all Cass remembered about that day was the color black, people crying, and rain.

The crowd was starting to thin as hugs and kisses tied travelers into family knots. Cass swallowed hard, hefting her bag onto her shoulder. Where could they be?

She sidled up to the check-in counter, clearing her throat. The clerk looked up from the pile of ticket coupons she'd been stamping. "Has anyone asked about a Cassandra McFerren? An older couple maybe?"

"Sorry." The young woman shrugged. "Why don't you try the white courtesy phone?"

Cass nodded and headed toward the dial-less telephone across the way. She startled as someone tapped her shoulder, and spun about to face a gray-haired man who was only slightly taller than she. He was kneading his hands together as if to keep them from flying away.

"Excuse me," he said. "I heard you say 'McFerren.' Are you Cassie?"

"Cass." She blinked at him, searching for something from her father's photo in the older man's features. "You have Dad's eyes, don't you? The same kind of blue."

The old man's face wrinkled into a grin. "Nope, he had mine. You're the only one in the world who's got his. My goodness, just look at you. All grown up."

Cass's cheeks felt warm. A breath of relief rushed out of her. How dumb could she be, thinking he wouldn't have met her plane? Dropping her things, she flung her arms about him and squeezed. But the hug he returned at last was stiff and awkward. Cass swallowed hard as she released him and stepped back, grabbing up her belongings.

"Where's your . . . where's Grandma?" she asked, mustering a familiarity she did not feel and he did not invite.

Ed McFerren cleared his throat, then straightened and retucked his short-sleeved white dress shirt. "She's back at the trailer. Resting, I hope. Said she wasn't feeling up to that walk from the parking lot."

"Oh." Cass tried to beat down the often-imagined fantasy of her only living grandmother, baking gooey-good chocolate chip cookies and taking her out for lunch and shopping at the mall. Maybe today was just an off day. Maybe she'd knocked herself out cooking and cleaning for Cass's arrival.

Her grandfather stared at her for a long moment, and his eyes welled with tears. He blotted them with a handkerchief and blew his nose. "Look at me, blubbering like a schoolboy. What's say we go get those bags of yours and hightail it home."

A half hour later, Cass's grandfather fumbled to

unlock the trunk of a white Lincoln Town Car, which gleamed like desert sand in the midday sun. Cass wondered whether he'd be offended if she offered to help, and decided to pretend not to notice. She gazed at the polished chrome trim, at the bumper, at the diamond-shaped dealer insignia that said McFerren Motors, Palm Springs, CA.

"Cool," she said. "You own the whole company?"

"I did for forty years. Right up till I retired and sold out to my nephew." He eased the trunk open and struggled with her suitcase.

Cass boosted it over the ledge, then tossed in her duffel bag. What nephew? she wondered. But what difference would it make if she knew? Her father's whole family were virtual strangers. A name would have meant nothing.

He slammed the lid. "Strong little thing, aren't you?"

Cass shrugged. She seldom thought of herself as strong. And never as little. She clambered in and buckled up, studying her grandfather's profile as he wove through traffic and onto Highway 360. His jaw was set in grim determination. What was going through his mind? Why didn't he talk, ask her about her trip, Mom, school—anything? Sitting there, his features as hard and pale as granite, he looked like an escaped face off Mount Rushmore.

She squirmed in the silence and at last turned toward the window, taking in the desert landscape that stretched south of the freeway, bleak and uninterrupted except for giant saguaro cacti that reached toward the sun. Two weeks in sunny Arizona, away from a snowy Iowa winter. Away from what's-his-name, Mom's latest resident jock, who—if he wasn't off skiing—would probably be hanging around the apartment, scarfing up all the Christmas goodies. So, what more could she ask for?

When her grandfather took the Greenfield turnoff and swung north toward Mesa, Cass pressed her lips together, gathered up her courage. "I-I was surprised to get your letter," she said. "And the ticket."

Her grandfather nodded but said nothing.

Cass's heart pounded against her chest. Say something! Why won't you talk to me? Her mind grappled with explanations. Maybe he wasn't feeling well. For all she knew, he could be in pain, dying of cancer. Or maybe he was just shy and used to his wife doing all the talking.

Cass hugged herself, felt her fat ooze between her arms. She grimaced and wished for the eighty-eleventh time that it would magically melt away. Then another explanation for her grandfather's coldness seized her, made her swallow hard. Maybe he was disappointed, now that he'd actually seen her.

As he turned off University into the Alta Mesa

Trailer Home Park for Seniors, she searched his face for a clue but found none. "I-I hope you're not sorry you invited me," she said.

Her grandfather braked to an abrupt halt. "Now what kind of nonsense is that? Why would we be sorry?"

Cass shrugged. Words evaded her.

"Takes time to love somebody," he said. "It'll come, but right now, we're the next thing to strangers."

Cass sank her teeth into her bottom lip, working off a crust of chapped skin. She tasted blood and blotted it with a tissue. He was right. Of course he was. How could she think they would love her *just because?*

The car jounced over a concrete speed bump and crawled down D Street. A small hand-lettered sign said: Welcome to Doggie Row. Walk and Bike at Your Own Risk. Each side was lined with nearly identical trailer homes set between covered slabs that doubled as carports and patios. Colored lights and Santa faces beamed down from the metal eaves and from an occasional saguaro; every bay window spilled holiday feeling into the street.

"So," Cass said, "what do you want me to call you?"

"Grandfather's fine."

Grandfather? Cass had to cover her mouth to contain her response. How about Mr. McFerren, sir? Is that formal enough?

"Or Ed's okay, if you prefer."

"Right." She nodded, but thought, If those are my only choices, I won't call you anything at all.

Grandfather-Ed pulled into the carport of space D-19 and Cass climbed out, her skin tingling. "Let's just leave everything," she said as he headed for the trunk. "First I want to meet my very own Grandma!"

Tripping up the steps, she knocked lightly on the door. Anticipation danced inside her.

"For Pete's sake, no need to knock," Grandfather said. "Go on in."

Cass opened the door a crack and a mediciny smell seeped out. A pathetic poinsettia parked on a small, round table had stained the carpet with its blood-red leaves. "Hello? It's me, Cass," she called into the dim interior.

A moment later she felt more than heard someone padding toward her from the back of the trailer. Leah McFerren squeezed through the narrow hallway, into the great room that encompassed kitchen, dinette, and living room, and flipped on an overhead light.

Instead of the petite, white-haired angel-grandmother of her imagination, Cass faced a massive, red-faced woman whose body appeared to have melted and settled around her hips. "My gift is here?" the woman said.

Gift? What on earth was she talking about? Cass turned to Grandfather, confused. But Grandfather said nothing, and her grandmother seemed to be looking to Cass for a response. Cass froze her face into a smile and endured Leah McFerren's appraisal. The woman raised one hand to her own cheek, massaging it absently.

"Oh, Lord, it's like seeing him rise up from the dead," she muttered with a disbelieving shake of her head that unloosed stray hairs from her salt-and-pepper bun. "Your mother should have warned me."

Cass inched forward and reached up to quickly kiss the woman's cheek. It felt like tissue paper and smelled strongly of rubbing alcohol. "Thank you for inviting me," she said.

Her grandmother's hand stroked the length of Cass's hair, but her lips kissed only air. "It was time, like the good book says."

Grandfather had apparently ducked out. He was standing in the doorway with Cass's nylon bag. "Where do you want this, Mother?" he said.

She indicated an afghan-covered couch beneath the bay window. "Cass, you call yourself?" Cass's grandmother waited for her nod. "So, how do you like our weather? Sweater weather, we call it. Don't know how you can stand all that bitter cold up north."

"All right, Mother. Ante up." Grandfather's eyes held the hint of a twinkle.

His wife sighed, fished in her pocketbook, then plunked several quarters into a crock on the counter. Cass frowned but said nothing. She figured that if they had wanted her to understand the strange custom, they would have explained it. Prying, she thought, would definitely be rude.

Instead, she searched for a more interesting topic of conversation. Weather was the last thing she wanted to talk about. Maybe they would loosen up a bit over a good meal. "Need some help fixing lunch?" she asked. "I'm a great cook. Or did Mom already tell you?"

"We don't really . . . talk." Her grandmother opened the refrigerator and stared into the white glare. "There's nothing much here except some potato soup and tongue." She shrugged apologetically while Cass choked down her response and remembered the box of chocolate raisins she'd packed in her suitcase. "I didn't know what you'd like. But you just sit down and make a list for Ed and I'll send him out to Smitty's."

"That's okay," Cass said. "I'm not really hungry."

She sidled up to the bay window and stared out at the identical trailer across the way in D-20. She saw movement inside and heard the muffled sound of music with a driving drumbeat. "Who lives across the street?" she asked.

The only reply was a frantic, clawing noise from the hall that made her reel about. As her grandmother opened the bedroom door, a yappy mop of a dog flew out and bounded toward Cass.

"Muffin need to go out?" Leah cooed through puckered lips. "Oo liddle baby need to make tinkle?"

Cass stifled a giggle. "I'll take him," she said.

"Her," Leah corrected. "You sure?"

Cass nodded. "What kind is she anyway?"

Leah shrugged. "Poor little thing had a broken leg when we found her back home. We nursed her from a pup. She's our baby, isn't she? Yes, she is." She fawned over Muffin, then handed Cass the leash. "She likes that rocky path at the end of the street. And make sure you let her go three times. She *always* goes three times. Always." Leah searched in a drawer and withdrew a plastic sandwich bag. "And if she poops, make sure you pick it up with this. Otherwise we've got trouble."

"Trouble?"

"A citation or some such nonsense," Grandfather said. "People around here got nothing better to do than go writing up their neighbors. A bunch of hooey, if you ask me."

"Now, Ed." Leah sighed. "You can't fight city hall. Rules are rules. And there's a waiting list a mile long, remember?"

"Maybe so, but I used to keep better track of my car inventories than I can all these crazy regulations. You darn near need a computer," Grandfather muttered.

"Don't worry," Cass said. "I'll stay out of trouble, and I'll take good care of her, . . . Grandma." No way she was going to call her "Grandmother" or "Leah." No way. She searched her grandmother's face for a reaction. But the older woman seemed more concerned about Muffin's welfare than about what her granddaughter called her.

Cass led the dog outside and down the steps to the street. "And don't let her get muddy," Grandma called. "See she stays out of that big puddle. And don't let her jump on anyone, hear me?"

"I hear you," Cass said to herself as she waved at her grandparents. Two weeks were beginning to seem like an eternity. And what if there were other rules they hadn't told her about? What would happen if she broke one unknowingly and got a citation? She wondered what the people around here did for fun, besides ratting on each other. Read the obituaries?

The distinct whine of heavy metal music was escaping from the trailer in D-20. Maybe someone had opened a door. Cass turned to stare at the trailer, as if sheer will could produce a friend for her in the big bay window bedecked with pale blue lights. When Muffin tugged on the leash, Cass sighed and started walking toward the rocky path and the huge puddle at the end of D Street.

Chapter 2

Jordy Sondel opened the side door of the trailer in space D-20 just far enough to get a good look at the dark-haired girl from across the street. She was short and kind of pudgy, or was it just that baggy sweatshirt she had on? Big deal. She was the first person under fifty that he'd seen in four days. That alone made her special. That, and the fact that she looked like she could use some holiday cheer. Perfect, he thought. So can I.

She stared hard at his grandparents' bay window and his pulse quickened. Had she seen him? Nah. Probably wondering where their Christmas tree was, he thought. Like the rest of the world.

"Come here, Rusty," he called over the latest Barrow Boys tape, tapping his thigh until his grandparents' Irish setter padded toward him. "Wanna go out?"

Rusty sat obediently as Jordy snapped the leash on. "Let's blow this pop stand, boy. What do you say?"

He slammed the door without locking it as two couples strode briskly by the trailer. One of the men doubled back and said, "Son, you got your name tag on? Didn't your people tell you you can't go out without it?"

"What's the difference?" Jordy said.

"Don't get smart with me. All I have to do is report you to the block captain and you'll have a citation. Maybe two. And that music isn't allowed either. Your people let you play it, or are they deaf?"

"No, sir." Jordy stared the man straight in the eye, and didn't even have to look up. He knew this guy, had met his kind back home, had seen him on TV. No matter what color they were or where they hailed from, guys like him always had a red neck.

"What's that supposed to mean?" The man called to his walking companions to wait for him, that he'd just be a minute.

"It means no, they don't let me play it and, no, they're not deaf," Jordy said, his chest tightening. *It's a free country. Just who does he think he is?*

"Well, we're not deaf either, mister. So it seems

to me, you'd better turn that trash off before your people come two points closer to getting kicked out of the park, hear me?"

Jordy scowled.

"Where are they, anyway? They're not supposed to leave kids unattended."

"I'm not a kid," Jordy said. "I'm almost fourteen."

"Like I said—a kid. Rules spell it out loud and clear. Now, where are they?"

Jordy shrugged. "How am I supposed to know? Maybe they're teaching another round dancing class. Or water aerobics. I can't keep track of everything they do."

The man pulled a stubby pencil and a folded envelope from his hip pocket. "All right. Just give me their names."

"Okay, sure thing." Jordy pursed his lips to keep them from cracking into a smile. "Methuselah and Shalamus." He groped for an equally outrageous last name.

The man rolled his eyes as he struggled with the spellings, then pointed to a carved redwood sign behind Jordy. "Ginsburg, right?"

"Yeah," Jordy said, sobering. "You got it." He'd forgotten that all residents were required to display identical plaques with their last names and outlines of their home state. Jeez, he was in for it now. Nana and Grandpa were going to be on his case full time if the guy carried out his threat. "Okay if I let the dog go pee?" Without waiting for the man's response, Jordy tugged on the leash, brushing past the others and into the street.

"See you pick up his mess," the man called after him. "Lousy dogs are crapping up the world. But we've got rules against that, too."

"Yeah, yeah, yeah," Jordy muttered to himself. "Ought to be rules against *you.*" He lengthened his stride to keep the walkers from catching up to him, then broke into a jog.

The girl had reached the edge of a pond-sized puddle left by yesterday's downpour and was letting her scruffy-looking dog sniff nearby. Several ducks bobbed in the water, nonplussed by the mutt's proximity. But when Rusty tugged and danced at the end of his leash, his hair ruffling like copper-colored feathers, they flapped off to the far side, keeping their distance.

Jordy drew closer, raking his fingers through the bleached streak in the front of his hair. He touched the tiny gold hoop in his left ear, willing himself to chill out.

"Hey," he said. "What's your name?"

The girl cocked her head as if debating whether to answer him. Jordy couldn't help but check out her eyes. He could tell a lot from someone's eyes, all he really needed to know. And this girl's were no exception. They were big and dark-lashed, the color of Seattle's sky after a good rain. But more than that, they were honest. He'd bet his drum set that she was no Jennifer.

At last she smiled. "My name's Cass. Cass McFerren."

Jordy slid his fidgeting hands into his pockets before they betrayed him.

"Ah," he said. His "Rock Stars Who Died Suddenly" research cards swam before his eyes. "Like in Mama."

"Mama?"

"You know. The old sixties pop star who . . . never mind." Jordy wondered whether she had a thing about her weight. Most girls did, even if they were sticks—and she was definitely no stick. Somehow he didn't think she'd be flattered to learn that Mama Cass, who supposedly had choked to death on a sandwich, had been grossly obese.

"So," he said, to fill the awkward silence, "what's in a name?"

"You tell me." She looked up at him, crinkling one eye.

"Huh?" Jordy felt his Adam's apple bounce and land. Was that a wink?

"Your *name,* silly. I told you mine."

"Jordan," he said. "Jordy, for short."

Her laugh tinkled like cat bells. "Gee, that's short all right. I bet you save all of one letter." She glanced over at her dog. "Did she just go?"

"Beats me." Rusty was panting and straining at the leash. Jordy unsnapped it and patted the setter's flank. "It's okay, boy. Go do your stuff."

At Jordy's urging, the dog bolted for the puddle, startling the bevy of ducks into the sky. Cass fliched from the mud that Rusty kicked up and grabbed for the little mop, whose yap would have made even corpses cringe.

"Grandma will kill me if Muffin gets dirty," she said. "Yours doesn't care?"

Jordy shrugged. Of course she did. Nana ragged him about everything—not rinsing his milk glass, wearing his Walkman earphones directly over his ears, feeding Rusty people food. But he was used to being hassled; it was all he ever got from Mom since the divorce. Made him feel right at home.

"She's supposed to go three times," Cass said. "Were you watching before?"

"Yeah, I was watching," Jordy said. "But not the dog."

Her cheeks pinked right up at that, and she grinned in response, making no move to put Jordy down with some smart remark. His insides unknotted as the realization seeped in that he'd won his mental bet. She was definitely *not* a Jennifer, too cool to permit herself feelings. Maybe he'd manage to pull this vacation out of the bag after all. . . .

Rusty loped through the mud and came tearing back toward them, his long pink tongue lolling out one side of his mouth. His hair was fringed with brown, and he shook himself with a fury that made even Jordy cower.

"Oh, no!" Cass wailed. "Just look at us!" She wiped some muddy flecks off her cheeks.

Jordy checked his urge to help her, to touch her face. "Nothing a good soak in the whirlpool won't fix," he said. "How about it?"

"Whirlpool?" She eyed Muffin or maybe the ground. "I couldn't. But . . . thanks."

"Why not? Come on, it'll be fun."

She shook her head. "I can't. Really. I've got stuff to do. You understand."

"Sure," Jordy teased. "Next thing you'll say is you've got to wash your hair."

"Well," she said, "don't I?" There was a sarcastic edge in her voice, but after a few moments her eyes began to dance.

"Yeah," Jordy said, cracking a smile, "I guess you do." Cass, indeed. She wasn't so tough. There was definitely a Cassie on the inside, crying to break out. For the first time since he'd arrived, it didn't matter so much that Hi and Dottie were off doing their thing instead of showing him the sights. Cass was like an early Chanukah present, just waiting to be unwrapped.

"So *that's* where you are!" Jordy turned toward the honey-coated voice behind him. "Do you know you left that tape player blaring? We could have gotten written up for that. And why didn't you lock the trailer? Someone could have made off with everything."

"Sorry, Nana. I was just walking Rusty."

"That's not what it looks like to me, young man." She glanced sidewise at Cass. "Just *think* once in a while, will you?"

Jordy sighed, turning his back on his grandmother. "I've got to go. See you later?"

Cass shrugged. "I don't know. Maybe. Good luck with your, uh . . ."

"Nana? You think *she's* bad? Grandpa's got fangs."

Cass giggled, batting her Seattle-sky eyes. Jordy caught Rusty on the rebound and snapped his chain on. Then he squared his shoulders, tossed back his hair, and led the muddy setter toward Nana. She didn't *have* to embarrass him in front of Cass, he thought. She could have waited until they were back at the trailer. But Mom was like that, too. He should be used to it.

"Thanks a heap," Nana said as he passed her the leash. "Seems you've found yourself a friend."

Loose hair the color of blanched almonds boiled about her face. Unless you looked at her hands, it was hard to believe she was sixty-two.

"Could be. She's staying in D-19. You know her grandparents?"

Nana raised one penciled eyebrow. "The McFerrens? No one does. They keep to themselves. Don't even come to the D Street potlucks. Sure beats me why they'd move to a place like this if they don't like to be sociable." She whirled about, showing off her hot pink and turquoise dress supported by a white net petticoat. "You didn't notice." She pouted. "I finished sewing at one this morning."

"It's nice," Jordy said. Well, the color was. The style made her look like a wind-up Kewpie doll. But it wasn't *her* fault that's what they wore to round dancing. For a grandmother, she had great legs. It was just weird that at her age she showed them off.

"You should see Grandpa in hot pink. He's getting daring in his old age."

Jordy shook his head. It didn't matter what Hi Ginsburg wore to dance class besides his silver toupee. The ladies loved him, couldn't wait to botch up a dance sequence so he could personally set them straight. Jordy should be so lucky when he was pushing seventy.

"What's he doing now?" he asked.

"Lining up records for tonight."

"Tonight?"

Nana ruffled Jordy's hair. "You remember. We're calling a dance over at Winterhaven. I'm sure we told you. If you're coming, it wouldn't hurt to get a haircut."

Jordy touched the back of his hair where it lapped over his collar. So it was starting to flip. Big deal.

"Ask Grandpa to take you to that retired barber over on G Street. He only charges two-fifty."

"That's okay," Jordy said. "Maybe I'll just stay home." He tried to sound offhand, but he had no intentions of letting anyone but Michael back home get near his hair with a pair of scissors.

"Don't be such a party pooper. My friend Lucille's been asking about you, wants you to save her a dance." Nana waved to a couple of passing bikers. "Besides, we promised your mom we'd show you a good time, and that's just what we're going to do."

Jordy sighed. A guy could have a heart attack having this much fun. He bet Dad was doing something exciting right now. Probably working on a big case, standing up for some little guy in court. "Doing the right thing"—that's how Dad described his life's work. Jordy liked that; he and Dad would have made a great couple of civil rights workers in the South. They shared a sense of outrage, Dad always said. But what else did he and Dad share now?

Not a home, that was for sure. Mom, Becca, and Amy had won that honor—not that they had had to compete. He couldn't help but wonder now whether "the girls" (as Dad called them) were trying to get rid of him over the holidays, or whether coming here to Arizona was supposed to be a special treat.

Outside the trailer Grandpa was sorting 45s on the front steps. Nana dropped Rusty's leash and the dog charged Grandpa, his tail whipping the air. Grandpa scrambled to his feet, grabbing Rusty's collar.

"Jordy, how many times do I have to tell you not to let him off the leash? Look at him! He's a mess. You think I have nothing better to do than give him a bath?" Grandpa's gray eyes sparked like flint.

"But he wanted to run," Jordy said. "You should have seen him."

"I see him. I'm seeing him."

"Don't worry. I'll give him a bath."

Grandpa loosened his bolo tie with one hand, the other still holding fast to Rusty's collar. "If *you* gave him a bath, then I *would* worry. Never mind. Just don't let it happen again."

Jordy sighed. What a bunch of bull! Listening to his grandparents put him down was like listening to Mom. Good thing he didn't believe everything he heard. He'd have given up on himself a long time ago. Even the new principal had him pegged as a troublemaker, and the man hadn't even been there six months yet. But challenging a teacher for making sexist comments was something to be commended, Jordy thought. Leave it to someone in authority to believe in blind obedience no matter what.

"Hiram," Nana said, "did anyone call?"

Jordy slipped past his grandparents and up the back steps that led to the master bedroom. His gaze fell on a green pleated curtain that was decorated with name pins: Hi Ginsburg, President, Four Squares. Dottie Ginsburg, Alta Mesa Aqua Fitness Staff. Hiram Ginsburg, Mesa Jewelry Workshop Staff. D. D. Ginsburg, Winterhaven R.D. Caller.

He flopped on their bed, imagining a new name tag for himself. Instead of "Jordan Sondel, Guest, D-20" it would say "Jordy Sondel, Tagalong of Four Squares President, Alta Mesa Aqua Fitness Staff, Mesa Jewelry Workshop Staff, and Winterhaven R.D. Caller" . . . except it wouldn't all fit.

He looked at their digital alarm clock, saw that the rest of the day still stretched before him. What great plans did Cass have that she couldn't go swimming? As far as he could figure, swimming was all there was to do. But only between the hours of noon and one or four and five, if you weren't a resident senior. Last year there had been shuffleboard, and he and Grandpa had had a few good matches. But this year, along with new equipment, the shed boasted a new sign: No Kids Allowed. Maybe Cass's grandparents were taking her to a movie or into town, the lucky stiff. What else was there?

Jordy rolled onto his side and closed his eyes. If Cass wasn't going to bail him out of this boring day, maybe a nap would. At least no one would be on his case—until he woke up. Maybe he'd replay his fantasy of leading a big, important protest march. There, things always turned out right: he made the front page, changed the course of history, won his father's respect. And you never know, he thought. By the time I wake up, maybe Cass will have changed her mind.

Chapter 3

Cass slunk into the trailer, cradling Muffin in her arms. If only she could sneak into the bathroom and wash her off, maybe Grandma wouldn't notice what that dumb Irish setter had done. Maybe she was too engrossed in stitching little flowers onto that hand towel.

"Did she go three times?" Grandma peered over the top of her glasses. "Because Lord knows we don't need any more accidents in here."

Cass nodded and kept edging toward the hall.

"What took you so long? I was getting ready to send Ed down after you."

"I met this boy from across the street. Jordy. Maybe you've seen him?"

Grandma shook her head. "You're awful young

to be messing around with boys. Just 'cause your mama's not here, don't think we're going to let you run wild."

"Me?" Cass blurted. "Don't worry, Grandma. I'm *not* interested." Grandma was a regular laugh-riot. *Mom* was the one who ran wild. As for Cass, boys ranked down there with "going on a diet and losing twenty-five pounds." Definitely something she thought about often, but nothing that was about to happen anytime soon.

Jordy had an earring, would you believe? And he'd bleached part of his dark hair blond. Totally freaky, even if he *did* have a cute smile. And what about that music he listened to? An obvious sign of an attitude problem, that was for sure.

Cass hurried into the bathroom before Grandma could stop her, closed the door, and ran the bath water. Muffin had started yapping and pawing to get out. Someone knocked impatiently. Cass twisted the button to lock the door.

"Let her out," Grandfather said. "Otherwise she's going to ruin the door."

"In a minute," Cass called. Her mind raced. "I can't . . . uh . . . go to the door right now."

Before anyone could pop the lock and barge in on her, she thrust the dog into the tub and rubbed her briskly with soap. Why hadn't she agreed to go swimming with Jordy? It would beat hanging around here all day, watching mold grow on the shower tiles. So what if swimming meant putting on her bathing suit? She wasn't out to seduce him, that was for sure. How uncool would it be to drop by his trailer later and tell him her plans had changed?

She was just rinsing Muffin when someone knocked again. "Cass, dear," Grandma called, "please let me in." There was an urgency in her tone. Was she going to be sick? Cass jumped up to unlock the door. Grandma hurried in, her housedress already raised about her hips.

"I'm so sorry," she said. "It's this colitis. And with only one bathroom, well, I can see we're going to have to adjust."

Cass wrapped Muffin in a towel, pressing herself against the wall of the closetlike room. She shrank from the overpowering smell, wishing she could reach for the can of air freshener without offending Grandma. Her heart beat faster as the older woman stared at Muffin, her mouth sagging open in surprise.

"What on God's green earth are you doing to my Muffin?"

"Giving her a bath," Cass said.

"But she's going to catch her death. We don't have the heat on." She fixed Cass with a hard stare, her red-veined nostrils flaring. "Next time ask before you do things. We've got our ways here, and the sooner you learn them, the happier we'll all be. Just put her down now, and put the towel over there." Grandma indicated one side of the bathtub, and Cass set the squirming dog down.

Good riddance, Cass thought, glad to be free of the shrill little thing. As she watched her grandmother coo over Muffin, a pang of jealousy nipped at her insides. Grandma treats her better than she treats me. Chagrined at the thought, she left the bathroom, changed into a dry sweater, and joined her grandfather in front of the TV.

"What are you watching?" she asked.

"Something about sharks. Fascinating stuff." Grandfather patted the seat cushion beside him, inviting her over. "Did you know that the great white has a jaw width of . . ."

Cass sighed, tuning out his boring recitation of details that was broken only by the narrator's monotone. Science was definitely *not* her preferred subject, even though she always mustered good grades. If I end up spending the entire vacation watching National Geographic specials, she thought, I'm going to scream. Even school is more exciting than this. She counted the days until her return flight on January sixth—fifteen. What in the world was she going to do until then? Raid the Mesa library and hole up on the couch with a pile of novels? She could have done better than that at home. At least there she and her best friend, Shelley, could have hit the rummage sales and worked on redoing Cass's room.

The blow dryer squealed from the bathroom, where Grandma was apparently trying to warm Muffin. Cass paced to the refrigerator and, realizing that she couldn't exactly help herself even if it *were* well stocked, back again. She looked out the window, trying to get a glimpse of Jordy across the way.

A handsome, silver-haired man, obviously his grandfather, was out in the carport, pulling 45s out of their jackets and examining them, apparently for dust. Piles of the old records littered his AstroTurf carpet. Maybe Jordy's grandparents were getting ready for a party. Or else a yard sale.

Cass cleared her throat to get her grandfather's attention. "Do you know the people across the way?"

He glanced behind him, then returned to his sharks. "Name's Ginsburg. Real active types. Come from up by San Francisco, I think."

"Are they nice?"

He shrugged. "Leah and me, we kind of keep to ourselves."

"Maybe we could invite them over," Cass said. "I could make my special beef Stroganoff. What do you think?"

"I doubt Leah'd feel up to it. She's got to kind of

take things easy like. What's say we just give it some time."

Cass tried to rein in her disappointment and chided herself for being so selfish.

"Is something wrong with Grandma besides colitis?" she asked. Surely that wasn't serious enough to make her avoid having dinner guests. Besides, Cass would do all the work. Grandma wouldn't even have to lift a finger.

"What?" Grandfather looked distracted—or maybe annoyed at her interruption. "No, she's going to be fine. You want to watch something? Here. We'll see what else is on." Cass shook her head, but he flipped through the television stations anyway and seemed not to notice when she ambled back to the bedroom to unpack. Why *had* her grandparents invited her? Neither seemed interested in getting to know her. They could have at least made a stab at conversation. Asked about school, her grades, anything. Heck, they hadn't even asked about Mom, their own daughter-in-law. She squeezed the last of her T-shirts into the lone empty drawer, feeling only slightly better for having gotten organized, then announced that she was going outside.

"Don't forget your name tag," Grandma called. "It's a silly rule, I know. Like you were a kindergartner and might forget who you are. But we're pretty new here. Best not rock the boat."

Cass grabbed it off the dresser, poking a finger in her haste to pin it on and get out of there. The trailer seemed to flinch as she slammed the back door. A three-tiered hanging basket of lemons and oranges swayed in the breeze. Across the street, behind the trailers, rose a white stucco wall, its top embedded with shards of green glass. Somewhere beyond it were deserts and sunsets and glorious red mountains. And with or without her grandparents, Cass intended to see them in person—not just on her beloved travel posters. After all, she reasoned, how could she be a travel writer if she never ventured out of her own yard?

As she started off toward the trailer park's main entrance, she saw Jordy's grandfather waving at her. He was balancing a stack of records, and when she returned the greeting, he tripped on the stairs. Records flew from their jackets and all over the ground as he struggled to break his fall. Cass raced to his side.

"Are you all right?" she said. "Here, let me help you."

He rolled over and sat on a step, examining his forearms. "Thanks. Nothing much hurt but my pride." He introduced himself as Hiram Ginsburg and told her to call him Hi.

"Cass," she said, and bent down to gather up the records. "I don't know how you want them." She set a stack beside him with an apologetic shrug. "You having a party or something?"

"Over at Winterhaven, a ways down University. Ever do any round dancing?"

Cass shook her head. She felt his eyes appraising her.

"Bet you'd be a natural," he said. "What do you say? Want me to ask your grandparents if you can come with us?"

"You mean it? That'd be great!" Surely Jordy would be there, too. Who could tell? It might be fun. And if the dance turned out to be a bust, at least they'd be bored together.

"Just wait till I redo these records," he said, "and I'll be right over."

A deeply tanned blonde woman in a purple bathing suit appeared in the doorway. "Oh, Hi," she wailed. "Are you still putzing around out here? My first graders sorted records faster than you do."

"He fell," Cass said, jumping to his defense.

The woman tapped her foot, her hands on her hips. "Mmm-hmm. And I'll bet you were watching a pretty girl instead of where you were going, right?"

Cass felt her cheeks flush; she eyed the ground.

"You're Jordy's friend, aren't you?" the woman

said. "I saw you out earlier with the dog. I'm Dottie."

"I talked her into coming with us to the dance," Hi said. "Why don't you go fix it up with her grandparents?"

Dottie nodded, clumped down the steps in her rubber thongs, and slipped into a white lace coverup that was hanging in the breezeway.

"Then I'm off to teach water aerobics," she announced. "You want to come?"

"Who, me?" Cass cringed at the idea. "Maybe some other time. I-I'm still getting settled in." Putting her bathing suit on was bad enough. But running and jumping in the water—jiggling *everything,* for Pete's sake—was even worse.

"Then come watch," Dottie said. "See for yourself how much fun it is. And bring your suit, in case you change your mind."

"Oh, I don't know."

"She who hesitates is lost," Hi called from the steps, where he was still resorting the records. "You don't know my Dottie."

Dottie smoothed Cass's hair away from her face, and Cass warmed to her touch. Had Mom ever played with her hair that way, absently but affectionately?

"What do you say?" asked Dottie. "I'll bet it's the best offer you've had all afternoon."

"Is Jordy coming?" Cass asked.

"Jordy? Please." Dottie laughed. "His idea of exercise is drumming on anything that'll make noise."

"Well, okay," Cass said. "Let me go grab my suit, and you talk to Grandma." She slipped in the back door as Dottie knocked on the front. Now where in the world had she stuffed that swimsuit? From the bedroom she could hear Dottie and Grandma talking.

"You sure she won't be a bother?" Grandma said.

"Not on your life. It'll do her good."

Cass scowled. The woman hasn't even known me five minutes and already she's out to make me lose weight. Why can't people just accept me the way I am? Like Jordy does. The thought caught her off balance. Maybe *that* was what she liked about him—despite his hair and his earring and his penchant for heavy metal. God, listen to me. Judging him by the way *he* looks. I'm as bad as the rest of the world.

Dottie hurried on. "Don't get me wrong. She's a beautiful girl. I just meant it would do her good to get out and meet some people, get a change of scenery. Matter of fact, why don't *you* join us?"

"I couldn't. Really. But it's nice of you to ask."

"Well," Dottie said, "if you change your mind, you know where we'll be."

"Do you have time for a cup of tea?"

Dottie tried to worm out of the invitation, but Grandfather jumped in, offering iced tea, already brewed, and Dottie did not refuse. Cass squeezed into her bathing suit, then put her clothes back on and accepted Grandma's offer of a towel from the linen closet.

"I'm ready," she said.

Dottie raised her tall glass as if toasting Cass's announcement. "Honey, would you do me a favor?" she said. "I left my towel on one of the kitchen chairs. Would you be a dear and go get it?"

Cass nodded and headed toward the front door. Through the window she could see Hi backing out in their minivan. "But Hi's just leaving," she said. "Won't I need a key?"

Dottie's hair bounced as she shook her head. "He must be going to set up for the dance, but Jordy's there. Just go on in."

Despite Dottie's urging, Cass knocked on the door. It pulsed to the drumbeat of Jordy's latest tape. She turned the knob. "Jordy? It's me, Cass."

There was no response, or if there was, it had been swallowed by the music. She inched into the room, wondering whether Rusty was the protective type, whether he'd come charging out of nowhere with teeth bared, primed for attack. A bold rainbow-print towel lay sprawled on a chair in the dinette.

As Cass started toward it, the breath caught in her throat and her hand flew to her mouth. Jordy stood beside the sink, wearing nylon jogging shorts and a cutoff T-shirt, oblivious to her presence. In his hand was a syringe and in his thigh, a needle.

Chapter 4

Jordy stuck the needle into his thigh and winced as he depressed the plunger. He'd hit a bad spot, and the insulin stung like crazy. He hesitated, bracing himself for the rest of the injection, then emptied the syringe. Nana had been right. He shouldn't have had that big bowl of ice cream with chocolate sauce for lunch. But at least she wasn't there to say "I told you so."

Breaking the needle off the syringe, he stuck it in its plastic cover and threw everything away. Then he swabbed the injection site with alcohol. When he glanced up, Cass was standing there, looking as if she'd just bumped into a junkie in a back alley. "What are *you* staring at?" he said.

Cass shook her head and grabbed Nana's towel.

"I-I'm sorry. I knocked. But I guess you didn't hear me."

"Guess not. Jeez, will you quit that?" Her eyes looked like a scared rabbit's. What did she think he was shooting? Heroin?

"I just came for your grandmother's towel." She turned toward the door. Jordy grabbed her arm. "What?" she demanded. "Don't! That hurts."

Jordy couldn't believe the look of shock in her eyes. He released her and backed off, his hands raised in surrender. She was acting as if he were some freaked-out druggie. But the way he figured it, as pudgy as she was, Cass was hardly one to judge a book by its cover.

"I thought you were different. You, of all people."

Cass tossed back her hair. "What's *that* supposed to mean?"

"You figure it out," Jordy said.

She stood there, biting her bottom lip. It looked raw enough to bleed. "I'm sorry," she said. "It's none of my business."

"You're right."

Silence hung over them like a teetering boulder about to roll. He wondered what he was getting so steamed about. If he wasn't careful, he was going to blow her right out the door—and there would go his hope of having someone to hang out with. For all he knew, his anger had already blown Dad out of all of their lives just as Becca maintained. "Look," he said, "I didn't mean to bite your head off."

"Yeah? Sure could have fooled me."

"You think I want the whole world to know I'm taking growth hormones?" he said, raking his fingers through his hair for convincing effect. "Jeez. I've got my pride."

"*Growth* hormones?" Cass frowned.

"Oh, yeah. I've probably grown six inches in the last few months." Jordy's own enthusiasm almost made *him* a believer.

"Hmmpf. Sounds like puberty to me," Cass said. She was staring at the insulin vial on the counter, probably wishing she had super-vision and could read the label from across the room.

"See? There you go again, calling me a liar. What can I say?" Jordy palmed the bottle offhandedly and deposited it in the fridge. "Believe what you want to believe."

"Don't worry. I will."

Jordy's anger bubbled up and spilled from his mouth, uncensored. "You really think you're something, don't you?" He felt suddenly taller, more powerful, like that Incredible Hulk character on rerun TV. "You just walk right in and assume I'm some kind of junkie. Unbelievable."

"Th-That's not true," Cass said. But she was

shrinking before his eyes. Just like his sisters and his mother back home, whenever he dipped into the poisoned anger-pot. He had to put the lid on before it was too late. Before she disappeared.

"That's okay. Let's just forget it." He forced a chuckle. "Maybe this'll teach me to turn the music down, huh?"

"Maybe," she said.

"Friends?"

"You got a better offer?"

Was she kidding? Yeah. Jordy shook his head. "Not today. But you can ask me again tomorrow."

"Don't worry," she said, flipping Nana's towel over her shoulder. "I will."

Jordy held the door and watched her beat a path across the street. What was her big hurry? He couldn't figure her out. One minute she was practically flirting with him, and the next, she was downright sarcastic. Girls. Could *anyone* ever understand them?

Moments later she emerged from the trailer with Nana. They were both carrying towels, laughing and talking as if they'd known each other for years. What in the world was going on?

Jordy slammed the door, and the whole trailer shuddered. He felt like kicking something, but, realizing he was still barefoot, reined in the impulse. The last thing he needed was a sore that wouldn't heal. Damn diabetes. One angry outburst could end up costing him a foot. It wasn't fair.

He grabbed his drumsticks off the coffee table and, using Grandpa's chair as a drum set, began practicing a new fill. Be creative, his teacher said. And don't stop. Jordy pressed his lips together, as if determination alone could push Cass from his thoughts and keep him on beat. But with every try, he flubbed his timing and stopped cold, and Cass's laughter floated in the air, teasing and chiding in the same breath.

When Grandpa returned from Winterhaven, the clock was pushing four. Nana breezed in a half hour later, planning aloud what she would make for supper. They'd eaten in every night since he'd arrived, and now Jordy wondered if the stripped-down, boring menus were on his account or whether his grandparents *always* ate stuff like skinless, boneless chicken, dry; microwaved zucchini, no cheese; and plain boiled rice. Yuck. There had to be more to life than always being in control.

Over supper Nana rattled on about her water aerobics class, how many people attended, all the nice comments she'd received. Jordy did not encourage her, keeping his eyes on his food instead, and, little by little, choking it down.

"That Cass McFerren is a lovely girl," Nana said. "Such a pretty face, don't you think so, Jordy?"

A tough bite of chicken caught in his throat and he coughed it up. "Yeah," he managed.

"Grandpa invited her to the dance tonight." She turned to her husband. "You told him, didn't you?"

"Did I?"

Jordy shook his head, making no effort to hide his scowl. "When were you planning to let *me* in on this, huh? When she walked in on me again?"

"Jordy." Nana patted his arm, but her patronizing tone made him pull away. When were they going to realize that his feelings mattered, that he had a right to be consulted about things? Whose life *was* this anyway?

"I'm sorry," Grandpa said. "Must have slipped my mind."

"Right." Jordy glowered at Grandpa.

"I'd like to be around to see how good *your* memory is when you get to be my age."

"Honestly, Jordy, we're not the enemy," Nana said. "I thought you'd be pleased. I just can't read you from one minute to the next."

Jordy stared at Nana, wondering why Mom's words were coming out of her mouth. What was Mom, a long-distance ventriloquist? How could she be up in Seattle with Amy and Becca and still be yammering at him here in Mesa?

"Don't look at your grandmother that way," Grandpa snapped. "Why must you *be* like this?"

Jordy snatched his dishes from the table and deposited them in the sink. Be like what? Angry? Jordy chuckled to himself. He had a list of reasons a mile long, if Grandpa cared to hear them. Diabetes topped it, of course. But that was just for starters. His parents' divorce ranked right up there, as did Dad not fighting for custody of him. Did Dad really think Jordy liked living with Mom and the girls, being the "man of the house"? Or was he too busy "doing the right thing" to want his son around? Maybe he's just a hypocrite, Jordy thought. Because he certainly isn't doing the right thing where I'm concerned.

"Jordy, I'm talking to you." Grandpa grabbed his shoulder and spun him around.

Jordy flung his arms up reflexively, breaking the older man's hold. Grandpa looked shocked as he raised his fists to protect his face. My God, he thinks I'm going to deck him, Jordy thought. Sobered by the realization, he backed away, the heat draining from his cheeks.

"Hey, Grandpa, hey," he said. "You've got the wrong idea." Rusty padded into the kitchen to nose around, and Jordy nudged him away. "Really. I wasn't going to hit you."

Nana got up from the table and stepped between them. "Of course you weren't, dear." She flashed

Grandpa a pointed look. "Don't you need to shave before the dance?"

Grandpa cleared his throat but he made no move to go.

"It's the way you touched me," Jordy said. He had to make Grandpa understand. "Something just snapped. I thought you were someone else. You don't believe me, do you? I can see it in your eyes. Why can't you believe me?"

Why should Jordy be surprised? Nobody ever believed him—not Mom or the new principal, not even his sisters. The only person who seemed to believe him was that shrink-guy Dad had made him see a couple times after the divorce. But then he was paid to believe him, wasn't he?

"Hi, leave it alone," Nana said. "Let it be."

Grandpa smoothed back a lock of synthetic silver that had fallen into one eye. "Who *are* you willing to hit?" he said.

Jordy sighed. How could he explain about Denny McClure and that whole gang always being on his case? There was the time Jordy had befriended a couple of Vietnamese kids and started a schoolwide donation drive to help furnish their homes and to provide warmer clothes. Gook-lover, they'd called him. They'd gotten the jump on him, too. And then there was that time he'd caught Denny and Company stealing out of the room where the sack lunches for the poor were kept. Another messy scene. After that he had wised up and watched his back. And when Jordy's rally for the homeless filled the school yard last month with what Denny called bums and winos, it was Denny who ended up in the dirt, listening to Jordy rag *him.*

"I give up," Grandpa said. "You try to talk to the kid and he's off somewhere. You touch him and he's ready to knock you flat. You sure he's not taking something besides insulin?"

"Hiram!" Nana branded him with a glare.

Jordy buttoned down inside. I'm okay. I'm not the person he thinks I am. Returning his grandfather's steady gaze, Jordy knew that he would say nothing, would give away nothing more.

"You're going to be just like your Uncle Ted if you don't watch out," Grandpa said.

Jordy could think of worse things. Just because Mom's brother had never gotten married or stuck with one job for long, was no reason to write him off. Maybe he was happy. Who could judge from the outside?

"Please," Nana said, "go shave so I can get into the bathroom."

Grandpa grudgingly headed down the hall while Nana stacked the dishes and filled the sink with soapy water. Jordy grabbed a towel. "What if I *did* turn out like Uncle Ted?" he said. "Would that be so terrible?"

Nana kept rinsing the same plate, avoiding his eyes. "Let's just say it would be a shame. You have so much potential, Jordy. But anger can destroy you, if you let it."

"Uncle Ted's not destroyed. He's doing okay." Heck, the guy tooled up to Seattle in a different sports car every time he came to visit, and he always took them out to Canlis's.

"That's *your* opinion. But I know my son. Everything's show-and-tell. Nothing's solid. Grandpa and I just can't keep bailing him out of every bad deal he gets himself into." She smiled ruefully and passed him the plate at last. "Who knows? Maybe we're getting selfish in our old age."

"Don't say that. You're not old," Jordy said.

"Well, I'm getting there."

Nana old? The thought was as preposterous as Jordy never getting fired up about things. Maybe he took her for granted, always assumed she'd be in his life to complain about. But what if she weren't? He swallowed hard, working the lump in his throat slowly down to his stomach, where it sat like unlit charcoal. She really *was* too young to talk like that. It gave him the creeps. He'd have done anything to beat back her words, but it was too late. Her admission hung in the air, casting its pall.

"What time's Cass coming?" he asked, anxious to change the subject.

"Seven. And you *will* be nice to her, won't you?"

"Yes, Mother." Nana elbowed him in the ribs. "I mean it," he said. "You sound just like her."

"I beg to differ. If anything, your mom sounds just like *me.*"

"Whatever," Jordy said. What was that expression? Like mother, like daughter? Mom and Nana could have coined it for themselves.

"I told Cass to wear a skirt, so you'd better change."

"You're sure she's still coming?" Jordy asked. Her last words *had* been pretty sarcastic. Maybe she hadn't forgiven him for that stupid outburst.

"Why wouldn't she be?"

"No reason," Jordy said, too quickly. He ducked Nana's probing gaze, concentrating on the glass he was drying.

"Did you two have words?"

"It's nothing," he said. "Just forget it." What was he doing? Living in a glass house, with every move he made open to public scrutiny? What he wouldn't give for a long walk in the desert—alone or with Cass, if she wanted to come. How he'd love to take off and just keep going!

Chapter 5

Cass had brought only one skirt to Arizona, a washed denim jean-style, and as soon as she entered the Winterhaven Trailer Park's social hall, she knew it was totally wrong. The women inside looked like upside-down peonies, their skirts bouncy, brilliant, and full. She hugged herself and slouched, as if that would make her less conspicuous.

"Jeez," Jordy said, "would you look at that?" He did not seem impressed. "Everybody matches."

"You mean like us?" He was wearing blue jeans, rips and all, which Dottie had nagged him about in the car on the way over.

Jordy laughed. "You got it."

At least *he* didn't seem to care that they stood out from the crowd, Cass thought.

Hi and Dottie stopped at the neighboring community's registration desk and filled out two stick-on name tags. Cass slapped hers on her sweater, while Jordy applied his to his thigh.

"You could have at least covered up some of those holes," his grandmother said. She seemed to be teasing, but Cass could read between the lines; Dottie obviously preferred a clean-cut image, which was too bad. Knowing Jordy the little she did, Cass guessed that there was no way he was ever going to measure up.

"Maybe next time we can talk your grandparents into coming," Hi said. "What do you think?"

"I don't know." Cass fidgeted with her rings, the pearl one Mom had given her when she had turned thirteen and the one she'd made at camp from a peach pit. "They need *something,* but I can't exactly picture them . . . dressed like this." Her gaze took in the men's bolo ties and mother-of-pearl–snapped shirts, the women's bouffant petticoats and matching hairdos. "No way," she said, shaking her head. "Not in a million years."

She tried to envision Grandma trading her formless housedress for the flirty red-over-black number worn by the registration desk lady. The sight, she thought, would be akin to an overweight, Old West madame wearing a tutu. And while Grandfather might look dapper in a silver-ornamented collar and stitch-creased slacks, she doubted that wearing lavender polyester with a gigantic turquoise belt buckle would loosen him up.

"You never know. They might surprise you," Hi said. "We'll see what we can do, okay?"

Dottie hustled him off toward the stage, where he was immediately intercepted by three women who began showing him problems they were having with various dance combinations. Their husbands stood to one side like mannequins as Hi took the women one by one through their paces.

"Unbelievable," Jordy said, shaking his head.

"What are you? Jealous?"

"Of Grandpa?" Jordy scoffed. "No way."

"Could have fooled me," Cass said.

"Yeah?" He scanned the room. "So, you want to sit down or what?"

Cass shrugged and followed him across the parquet floor to a row of folding chairs along one wall. Dottie, a microphone hung around her neck, was welcoming the dancers.

"I don't know why you wanted to come," Jordy said. "This is going to be bor-ing. Just thought I'd warn you."

"It *can't* be as bad as staying back there with my grandparents." She bit her lip, wondering whether she should say more. "They're nothing like I thought they'd be, that's for sure."

"You talk like you never met them before."

"Maybe that's because I never did," Cass said, figuring one time at Dad's funeral didn't count. "Not only that, but I never even *heard* from them before."

"Really? Why not?"

"Because they're my dad's parents, and he died when I was three."

"So?"

Jordy's response caught her off-guard, and she knew her face showed it. "So . . . so I've always lived in Iowa. And they've lived wherever, California, here. It's not like they could just bop over and visit, you know." She wondered why she was getting so upset.

"Yeah, but . . ." Jordy flicked back his hair. "Jeez, you'd think they could at least write or pick up the phone. That *is* kind of weird, don't you think?"

Cass tried to push aside the memory of all the times she'd wondered the same thing herself, and more. Didn't they love her? Maybe she'd done something wrong at the funeral. But how could she have? She was just a little kid.

She blew out a long breath. "Look," she said, "that's just the way it was, okay?"

"Okay," Jordy said, raising his hands. "Okay already."

Cass fidgeted in her chair. Did Jordy intend to sit

here all night, poking his nose in her business, or was he going to ask her to dance? Hi had just put a new record on, and Dottie was calling out strange words like *whisk* and *wing, sidecar* and *butterfly.* Though a few couples looked lost in the dance pattern, most were moving in unison around the circle.

"Well," she said, "are we going to try this or not?"

"Are you kidding? I don't know how to do this stuff."

"You think *I* do?" Cass said. "Maybe we could just fake it."

"You want to dance? Go talk to Grandpa."

"But—"

"He invited you, didn't he?" Jordy said.

Cass eyed the exit across the room, wishing she could flee. He was right. Maybe he didn't even *like* to dance, and his grandparents had used her to get him to come. She'd been so hopeful that they might have some fun. . . .

"Hey." Jordy touched her hand, pulling her out of her thoughts. "I didn't mean that like it sounded. I'm glad you're here."

Cass blinked up at him. "You are?"

"Sure," he said. "Beats talking to myself. Just kidding."

Cass punched his shoulder playfully. "You mean it *doesn't* beat it?"

"Touché. You want to take a walk?"

"Is it okay?"

"It's okay with me."

Cass laughed. Whose permission did she think she needed? Mom's? Of course *she* wouldn't approve. Jordy was too wild-looking, nothing like the model-perfect guys Mom hung out with. But so what? That didn't mean he wasn't nice.

Jordy tugged her off the chair and steered her by the elbow across the room. With the sunset, winter settled over Arizona, frosting the breeze. Cass shivered inside her sweater, wondering why she hadn't thought to bring a coat. She saw Jordy clutch his jean jacket closer at the throat as he headed toward the L-shaped pool. Steam was rising off the surface. A nip of chlorine hung in the air.

"L-Looks warmer in there," Cass said.

"You cold?"

"You kidding?"

Jordy peeled off his jacket and draped it over her shoulders. "See if that helps."

"Thanks." She doubted whether the jacket would even fit and was grateful he didn't encourage her to put it on. Jordy had to be freezing, but he was trying hard not to show it.

"So," he said, thrusting his hands into his pockets, "it's you and your mom and . . ."

"That's it." That was enough. Mom was a bigger kid than she was, and Cass felt more like the mother than the daughter. "What about you?"

"I've got two little sisters," he said. "And my mom, of course." Ducking his head, he muttered as if to the concrete, "My old man split last winter."

"I'm sorry." It wasn't as if his dad had died, but by the hangdog look on Jordy's face, he may as well have.

"No big deal."

Yeah, right, Cass thought, but she said nothing. Music drifted out of the hall with Dottie's cues, and curled around them. Would it be so hard to try and follow along? It would sure beat standing out there, pretending not to freeze. Catching the rhythm with her feet, she began waltzing in place, hoping Jordy would get the hint.

At last he said, "You really want to do this stuff, huh?"

Cass nodded.

"And you don't care if we make complete fools of ourselves?"

Cass hesitated. Of course she did. But they were bound to anyway, no matter how well they danced, what with her dumb skirt and his ripped jeans. "Why should *I* care? I don't know these people," she said at last. "Do you?"

"Are you kidding? Okay then. Come on. Let's go give them something to talk about." Linking arms with her, he led her back inside.

Her cheeks burned and the welcome warmth made her shiver as she returned his jacket. She hesitated outside the circle of dancers, gathering up her nerve as Dottie announced the next song. Jordy caught her hand and tugged her into position between a couple in pink and white and another in aqua.

"Aren't you Hi's grandson?" one of the women said. "I was just asking about you last week, whether you were coming down this year. I'm Lucille, remember?"

Jordy bobbed his head without conviction. "This is my friend, Cass. She's from Iowa."

Lucille nudged her husband and winked at them both. "How long are you staying, dear?"

"Till the sixth," she said.

"At Alta Mesa?" At Cass's nod, Lucille's penciled eyebrows knit together. "Honey, I don't think you *can.*"

"What do you mean?" Cass said. "My grandparents sent me the ticket. Why can't I?"

"I think they only allow kids through January first. Best I can tell, Alta Mesa's real strict about that, too. Grounds for eviction, is what they say. Not like here at Winterhaven. But then we don't have a big waiting list of people wanting to get in, either."

"So?" Jordy said. "What does that mean?"

"It means, hon, that Alta Mesa can afford to be picky. If they kick somebody out, they can pretty much fill the place with folks they want." Lucille shrugged apologetically. "Have your grandparents recheck their handbook. Or, better yet, talk to the manager."

"I will," Cass said. "Thanks, I think."

Lucille turned to her husband. "Don't they look cute together?" she said. As Hi dropped the needle onto the next record and restarted it, she called over her shoulder, "You two have fun now."

Jordy pulled Cass into dance position and whispered, "That's a bunch of bull! They can't kick you out. Or your grandparents."

She worked on her bottom lip. "Are you sure about that?"

"Think they can violate your civil rights just because you're a kid? No way. What are they going to do, throw you out in the street?"

Jordy began leading her around to the music with a stiff box step, his hazel eyes trained on her face. Other couples whooshed past them in a rustle of skirts, but he seemed not to notice.

"I don't want to make any trouble," she said. "They hate me as it is."

"I doubt that."

"You don't know them," Cass said. "They can't even hug me like they mean it. And all they talk about is the weather and dumb stuff like sharks."

"Grandparents." Jordy shook his head. "You've got to train them, that's all. Otherwise they try to lay all their trips on you. Believe me. I know what I'm talking about."

Cass stumbled over his feet and mumbled an apology. Hi and Dottie were wonderful grandparents. What could Jordy possibly have to complain about? She looked up at him questioningly, but his expression held no clue.

"Look," Jordy said, "let me ask Nana to check this out first. Otherwise your name's going to get out and the manager will be watching you like a hawk. Anyway, you never know. Maybe she can use her connections."

"That'd be great. Thanks."

"Don't thank me until it helps," Jordy said. "I don't know about you, but there's no way I'd let them kick *me* out without a good fight."

"So when are *you* leaving?"

"On the first." Jordy shrugged. "Maybe your school starts later than ours."

Cass sighed. Why hadn't her grandparents known about the stupid rule anyway? They'd moved to Alta Mesa at the end of last spring. Surely they'd had time to read that handbook Lucille had mentioned. "Well," she said, "I guess I'll just have to pin my hopes on Dottie, huh? What else can I do?"

"Are you asking *me*?"

"Sure, why not?"

"Well . . ." Jordy looked thoughtful. "If talking doesn't work—I mean if the guy won't budge—we could always start a petition. No sweat. I've done it lots of times. And if that doesn't do any good, we could stage a sit-in in the rec hall. That'd get 'em."

The music had stopped and Cass went through the motions of applauding, as the others were. "I don't know," she said, wishing she could share Jordy's conviction.

"Well, *I* do. You can't just let 'em dump on you. Believe me. I know what I'm talking about."

"Yes," she teased, "you said that before. Are you always so sure of yourself?"

"Yep." Jordy grinned. "I'm the only one who never let me down."

"Must be nice." Cass embraced herself as if to ward off the way he was looking at her. She felt transparent. How did *he* know that she let herself down all the time? Every Monday morning, for starters, when she'd break her diet after only three hours. Why couldn't she just put her mind to it and buckle down, the way she did with studying and taking care of their flat?

A new record blared through the speakers, a peppy line dance called "Amos Moses." Couples were spreading out across the floor, laughing about how long it had been since they'd tried this and what a disaster it was bound to be.

"Come on," Jordy said, maneuvering her into a free space. "Sounds like we can mess this one up good and no one'll even notice."

Cass copied the man next to her, quickly picking up the series of dance steps. "Atta girl," he said. "You got it now."

Jordy was clapping his hands and whooping at appropriate changes in the tempo. Cass's cheeks flushed with effort. Sweat trickled down her neck and chest. But for once, she didn't mind. On the turn steps she reveled in the swish of hair about her face, and spun toward Jordy, laughing. Grabbing her hands, he twirled her about in circles, faster and faster, until the other dancers blurred like a kaleidoscope, until, breathless, she begged him to stop.

Chapter 6

Jordy stood outside the trailer, holding a brown paper bag while Nana nestled a chunky candle in its sand-filled bottom. Why should *he* care that today was Christmas Eve? To him is was just plain old December twenty-fourth. "I don't see why you go through this baloney every year," he said. "It's not as if we celebrate Christmas, you know."

"This has nothing to do with Christmas," Nana said. She tucked her hair behind her ears, then leaned over to add sand to several more bags.

"Oh, yeah?" Jordy stared at her, incredulous. "Then why do we wait till Christmas Eve to perform this charming little ritual?"

"You don't have to be sarcastic," Nana said.

"How do you think it'd look if we were the only ones without luminarias?"

Jordy glanced up and down D Street. Brown sacks lined both sides, except right across the way. "The McFerrens don't have any," he said. "Maybe you two could start a middle-of-the-road tradition." When Nana frowned, he added, "That was a joke, you know? As in ha-ha?"

Nana nodded, forcing a smile, and handed Jordy another bag. "This is their first winter here. Maybe they didn't read their newsletter."

"That's not *all* they didn't read," Jordy muttered.

"Which reminds me," Nana said. "I talked to the manager about Cass's problem. But you're not going to like what he had to say. All he needs is one little complaint and he'll have to send Cass home, and maybe even—"

"Don't tell me." Jordy groaned. He knew talking to the manager wouldn't help.

"Well," Nana said, "I can see his point about making exceptions. You do it for one, you've got to do it for all. And then what would happen?"

"Beats me." Jordy made no effort to rein in his sarcasm.

"Jordan!"

"What about due process, huh? What about that?"

"Since when are *you* a lawyer?"

Jordy scowled. He bet he knew a lot more than she thought he did. Just because his grades stunk didn't mean he wasn't smart. He learned what interested him, and what he needed to know—like stuff about diabetes. The rest was just a game, *their* game, and right now, he didn't feel like playing. Maybe he would feel differently when his game scores counted. Maybe when he hit high school. Maybe then.

"Jordy," Nana said, "this is really none of our business. I suggest you let the McFerrens handle it themselves, okay?"

Jordy did not reply. One complaint, huh? Who could guess how many small minds there were lurking around Alta Mesa, just itching to report somebody? Already he could think of one guy—the walker. That nosy creep was a regular citizen on patrol. Poor Cass. If she didn't get this ironed out quick, her visit was going to end in disaster.

Nana added a candle to the last bag, and Jordy helped her ferry the luminarias to the beach-towel–sized rock garden in front of the trailer. "I've got to go talk to Cass," he said.

"Okay, but remember what I said. And tell them about the luminarias, will you? Everything they need is up at the rec hall."

Jordy rolled his eyes.

"I mean it," Nana said. "What if everybody did

their own thing? None of the tour buses would even bother to drive in and look at our lights."

"And that would be the end of the world, right?"

Nana pressed her lips together and blew out a long breath. "Just be home to shoot by six," she said. "And we'll do Chanukah before the Santa wagon comes around."

"All right already." Jordy felt a storm boil up inside him. Do Chanukah. The expression rang in his ears. It was a religious holiday, for God's sake. A festival of freedom. And technically it had been over for a week. But for his grandparents tonight was more convenient. They'd fry up some latkes, light a few candles, and open the gifts everyone else was saving until Christmas morning. Do Chanukah. What a joke! Just get out of here, he thought. Leave me alone. He turned his face toward the dying sun, waiting for his anger to ebb, for Nana to go inside.

But instead of subsiding, the feeling grew. What was he *really* mad about? Nana telling him to be back by six? Yeah, that was it. He knew when he needed to "shoot," so she could just get off his back and stop trying to control his diabetes for him. It was *his* problem, not hers. Why couldn't she and the rest of the world butt out and let him take care of it?

At last he heard his grandparents' trailer door close. As he mounted the steps to the McFerrens', Muffin began to yip. When Cass's grandmother opened the door, the pungent smell of garlic forced itself out around her bulky frame. Drying her hands on the skirt of her long-sleeved apron, she reluctantly invited him in.

"Cass," she called, "that boy from across the street is here."

Cass appeared in the hallway, one cheek unusually pink. "Jordy," she said to her grandmother. "I told you a million times." She turned to him, holding a hand to her face, and smiled. "Hi."

"No, *Jordy*," he said. "Hi's my grandpa. I told you a million times."

"Very funny." Cass rolled her eyes and let her hand drop to her side. The red beginning of a pimple stared from the middle of her well-scrubbed cheek. "What are *you* looking at?" she snapped.

"Nothing." He cracked his knuckles, first one hand, then the other. If *his* face had just broken out, he guessed he'd be mad, too. She'd meant nothing personal. He cleared his throat, glancing uneasily at Cass's grandmother puttering about the kitchen. "So," he said, "did you tell them what Lucille said?"

Cass shook her head and hushed him.

"Why not?" he whispered. "What are you waiting for?" Jordy felt Mr. McFerren's eyes peeking above his newspaper and self-consciously fingered his earring. "Nana checked and it's like Lucille said. One complaint buys you guys automatic eviction."

Cass's blue eyes widened. "Seriously?"

"You think I'd kid about a thing like that?"

Cass hung her head. "I just haven't found the right time," she said. "Maybe tomorrow, after we open our presents."

"Yeah. And tomorrow you'll say 'tomorrow' or 'the next day.' It's not going to get any easier, you know."

"I know. I just thought if I had more time, I could work out a solution."

"Uh-uh. No way. We've got to do something. You can't just sit around and wait for them to kick you out."

"Maybe we should cool it, be a little more patient." But Jordy could sense her resignation, could see defeat in her eyes already, and it ticked him off. No friend of his was going to give up without a fight. "Maybe the manager will change his mind."

Fat chance, Jordy thought, but he didn't say it. "Look, what can you do? Go stay in a motel?" His voice rose in exasperation. "For five nights you're talking big bucks."

"Did I hear you say 'Bucks'?" Mr. McFerren said, setting aside his newspaper. "So you're a Milwaukee fan, huh?"

"Uh, not exactly." Jordy searched Cass's face for a clue as to what her grandfather was talking about.

Baseball? Hockey? But it was obvious from her blank expression that she was no sports fan either.

"Pity. That club can use all the fans they can get." Mr. McFerren rose from his chair and straightened his sweater vest. "I saw your grandmother setting out decorations," he said. "You folks all ready for Christmas?"

"Not really," Jordy said. "We're Jewish."

"Oh," Mrs. McFerren said from the kitchen. Jordy wondered whether what he heard in her voice was surprise or apology. "I didn't know. I mean I—we—just figured . . ."

"With the decorations and all," Mr. McFerren added lamely.

Jordy struggled to put the derailed conversation back on track. "Don't ask *me* why Nana puts out those luminarias," he said. "I guess because everyone else does."

"Are *we* supposed to?" Cass asked.

Mr. McFerren shrugged. "They send us so darned much stuff to read around here, I don't even bother. Except for Leah's bingo every Monday, we keep pretty much to ourselves."

"I doubt it's a *rule* or anything," Jordy said pointedly. "I mean, nothing's going to happen if you *don't* put them out." He narrowed his gaze at Cass, hoping she'd get the message.

"But now we're the only ones who don't have them." Cass wrinkled up her mouth. "What will people say?"

Who cares? Jordy thought. You could guess your head off all day about what people *might* say and be totally wrong. And in the meantime, you've done something you didn't want to do in the first place. Was he the only one who understood that?

"I'm not going to lose any sleep over it," Mr. McFerren was saying. "But if you are, honey, then you may as well go do something about it."

Jordy wondered whether Cass would rope him into helping her make a set of luminarias. She was kneeling on the couch, staring out the window, apparently deciding what she wanted to do.

Jordy shivered, wondering why the McFerrens' trailer was so cold. Maybe they were having problems with their heating system. Didn't Cass even notice? After a few moments, Cass' grandmother eased a golden-brown turkey from the oven and basted it. Fat crackled in the roasting pan as the liquid made contact. Her face flushed as she nudged a stray wisp of hair off her forehead with her wrist. "Cass, help me here, will you?" she said. "I'm not feeling so well."

Cass leaped up from the sofa to relieve her of the roaster, while Jordy rolled a chair over from the dinette. The cushion hissed as she sat down, rubbing her chest and breathing hard. Mr. McFerren grabbed a pillbox off the table and handed her a tiny white tablet that looked like saccharin.

"Under your tongue," he said. "That's the way."

"Are you okay?" Cass said.

Her grandmother held up one finger, and it was several minutes before she assured them that she was all right. "Maybe I'll go lie down," she said. "Do you think you can finish making supper?"

"No problem." Cass eased Mrs. McFerren out of the chair and helped her down the hall. "Don't worry about a thing," she said. "I'll take care of you."

As Jordy watched them disappear into the bedroom, a knot rose in his throat. At least Cass was making progress. Mrs. McFerren had asked for her help and accepted it. That was a start. All his grandparents ever did was criticize.

Mr. McFerren patted him on the back. "She'll be all right," he said. "But having Cass here sure is a comfort. More than she'll ever know."

Jordy could not contain the question: "Then why don't you tell her?" From the shocked look on Mr. McFerren's face, Jordy knew he should have kept his thoughts to himself. But what the heck?

"Tell her?" Mr. McFerren rubbed his hands together as if he were washing them. "Why would I want to do that?"

"So she'd know how you feel about her," Jordy said. "So she'd know you care."

"Don't be ridiculous. She knows that."

"How could she?" Jordy blurted. "In all those years you never even wrote or called."

Mr. McFerren winced as if he'd been slapped. When he recovered, he shuffled over to a gray metal file cabinet by the TV and pulled out a rubber-banded stack of letters. "Not that it's any of your business, but what do you call these?"

The envelope on top, addressed to Miss Cassandra McFerren, was marked "return to sender" in black felt pen. Jordy flipped through the pile. "They're all the same," he said.

"That's right." Mr. McFerren replaced the letters in the drawer. "Our daughter-in-law's doing, I'm sure."

Jordy's pulse quickened. "But Cass should know," he said.

Mr. McFerren shook his head. "Some things are better left unsaid. Kelly wasn't much of a wife, to my way of thinking, but she's done all right by Cass. No sense spoiling things between them, you hear?"

Jordy swallowed his protest. He could tell Cass whatever he pleased, and he intended to. But he didn't have to admit that to her grandfather. No sense waving a red flag in the old guy's face.

The sound of a sliding door made him look toward the bedroom. Cass padded into the great room, her dark hair falling around her face in waves. "She's almost asleep," she said. "But I think I'd better stick around. Who cares about those candle-things anyway?"

Jordy made a fist and punched the air. "Right on," he said. Then, "Hey! What time is it anyway?"

"Almost six," Cass said. "Why?"

"No reason." Jordy shrugged. "I probably ought to wear a watch 'cept it's against my religion."

"Yeah, I'll bet."

Jordy backed toward the door. "Well," he said, "Merry Christmas."

Cass opened it and followed him onto the top step. "Merry Chanukah. Is that what you say?"

"Close enough." Jordy touched her cheek, the one with the pimple she'd tried to hide earlier. She was okay just the way she was. Why couldn't she believe that? "Catch you later," he said. "I've got a present for you. Kind of."

He clattered down the stairs and turned to wave. A sprig of mistletoe was hanging in the doorway. Was that why Cass had followed him out? He cursed himself for not having noticed it sooner. There was no way he could turn back now. It'd be too awkward.

Chapter 7

Cass spied Jordy across the crowded social hall. He was sitting in the front row with a bunch of little kids at his feet and two others in his lap. She pressed her lips together to suppress a giggle. He hardly seemed like the Pied Piper type, but there he was, spinning stories with his hands, holding the kids' attention until the Christmas Eve pageant began at eight.

"You'll be all right if I go back to the trailer and stay with Leah?" Grandfather asked.

Cass nodded, pointing out Jordy. "I'm sure he'll walk me back," she said.

"What's *he* doing here? I thought he said he was Jewish."

Cass shrugged. So what if he was? There was nothing else to do around here tonight. Besides, knowing Hi and Dottie, they were probably *in* the show. So why wouldn't Jordy be there?

"Tell Grandma I hope she feels better," she said, kissing her grandfather awkwardly on the cheek.

She watched him shrink off into the night, then made her way toward Jordy. As she drew closer, she caught the end of his story about Santa going to a Jewish boy's house by mistake.

The girl on his lap regarded him seriously, holding his cheeks between her chubby hands. "Santa never goes to your house either, does he?" she said.

Jordy shook his head.

"Never ever?"

"Never ever." The finality in his voice almost made Cass feel sorry for him. What would December be like without Christmas trees and colored lights and cookie exchanges? It was the only month that Mom really behaved like a mother—cooking, shopping, and entering into family traditions with enthusiasm. But how could Jordy miss things that he'd never experienced in the first place?

With a finger to her lips, she tiptoed up behind him and slipped her hands over his eyes.

"Sarah?" Jordy guessed.

The girl on his lap squealed and shook her head.

"Lindsay?"

"No way," said an older girl who was sitting at his feet.

"Don't tell me," Jordy said, his hands creeping up to feel hers. "It's Jennifer!"

No one said anything and Cass jerked her hands away. "Who's Jennifer?" she demanded.

"Oh, look, guys," he said. "It's Cass. I bet *she'll* tell you a story, won't you, Cass?" Shooing a boy off the chair beside him, he bobbed his head as if to convince her. "Come on, now. Don't wimp out on us."

Cass sat down, nailing him with a look. Who in the world was Jennifer? And why did Cass even care? "You want another story, huh? What was wrong with the one Jordy told you?"

"Nothing was *wrong* with it," Jordy snapped. "It's over, that's all. And we've still got ten minutes to kill."

"How would *you* know?" she teased. "You don't even wear a watch."

"So what? Is that a crime?" Color rose in his cheeks.

Oh, give me a break, Cass thought. You don't have to get so defensive; I was only kidding. She wished she could reel in her words, tell him to just ignore her stupid sense of humor. Shivering inside her sweater, she hugged herself and wished for some private place to which she could escape. "That was supposed to be a joke," she said at last. "No reflection on you. Honest."

Jordy's expression softened. "Then you're not mad?"

"Mad?" Cass blinked. "About what?"

"The mistletoe," Jordy said. "What else?"

"*What* mistletoe?" Cass pretended she'd never even seen it in the doorway. She was amazed to realize he'd been feeling guilty for the last couple of hours about not having kissed her. Unbelievable.

"Never mind." Jordy blew out a short breath. "Maybe we should just shut up and watch the show, before we both die of foot-in-mouth disease."

"You got it," Cass said, swallowing her own relief. He was her best hope for a fun vacation. The last thing she wanted to do was keep him at arm's length with her sarcasm. Turn it down. Just be yourself. Why was the thought so scary? She took the chair beside him and launched into her own rendition of "'Twas the Night before Christmas," which the children loudly corrected whenever she gave them the chance.

At last Alta Mesa's manager took the stage to welcome the residents and their visitors. As the kids scurried off to join their respective sets of grandparents, Jordy breathed an audible sigh of relief. "Good," he said, his eyes laughing. "Alone at last."

"Right." Cass nudged his arm. "Are Dottie and Hi in this?"

"How'd you guess?" He sounded bored already.

"Come on," she whispered. "It can't be *that* bad. How long do these things last?"

"Forever. Want to split?"

"And do what?" Cass said.

Jordy shrugged. "Whatever you want. It wouldn't take much to beat a bunch of old ladies tap dancing."

Cass clapped her hand over her mouth to contain a giggle, imagining the act Jordy described. She could care less about watching the pageant, but walking out once it began was another story. If Hi and Dottie saw them, they might take it personally, and Cass did not want to hurt their feelings. "Well," she whispered, "if we're going, we'd better go. One by one. Like we're heading for the bathroom."

"You got it," Jordy said. "Meet you out back by the pool."

Cass ducked to avoid the spotlight and hurried toward the restrooms, then slipped outside. Steam curled up from the whirlpool, spiking the air with chlorine. Her pulse raced as she huddled in the bathhouse's shadow. At last the door opened and Jordy hissed her name into the darkness.

"Here I am," Cass said, stepping forward. "Where to now?"

Jordy steered her by the elbow toward a tall iron

gate, which he opened soundlessly. "Come on!" He tugged her hand, quickened his pace.

Cass struggled to keep up, half running, half walking. "Where are we going?" she asked. A dark field stretched before them. Its farthest edge shone in the sliver of moonlight. "What *is* that?"

"You'll see." Jordy glanced back and slowed to a stroll. "Better watch out for rocks."

"I was afraid you were going to say rattlesnakes." Cass picked her way across the field, still letting him guide her. His touch was reassuring in the near darkness. Soon an irrigation canal bisected their way, and Jordy led her along the levee. They walked on in silence for several minutes, and Cass kept wondering whether she should say something—anything—to fill the quiet. But nothing came, and she contented herself with admiring the orange groves that rose up on the other side of the canal.

"How's your grandma?" Jordy said at last. "She okay?"

"I guess. Whatever it was, she didn't want to talk about it."

"That figures."

"What's that supposed to mean?" she asked.

"Grown-ups *never* want to talk about anything important. What do they think, we're stupid or something?"

Cass did not understand where he was coming

from. What wasn't *he* telling her? She wondered whether she should tell him what she had just learned about her grandparents, that they were trying *not* to make small talk anymore. After dinner Grandfather had anted up seventy-five cents for the mysterious crock after making some comment about the wind chill in Iowa. When Cass had asked why, Grandma explained their self-imposed fine system and how they were donating the kitty to their church's "Save-a-Child" fund. Maybe *that* would impress Jordy, she thought.

But he didn't give her a chance. "I mean, do they think we don't see what's going on?"

"What *is* going on?" Cass said. Her pulse quickened. "You think my grandmother's really sick, don't you?"

Jordy stopped walking and turned to face her. "Yeah, maybe. But it's not just her. It's everything. Why can't they come right out and *tell* us what's going on? We can handle it."

Cass struggled to connect the incident to something broader. Were Hi and Dottie keeping something from him? What about his parents? "Are you being paranoid or what?" she said.

"I wish." Jordy picked up a stone and tried to skip it down the canal but it plunked to the bottom instead. "Divorce is the pits."

"Oh." They'd sprung it on him; *that's* what he

was talking about. "I guess I wouldn't know about divorce."

"I guess you wouldn't know about a lot of things," Jordy said, but not unkindly.

She wondered what he meant. If he thought she was some hick from Iowa, he had another think coming. She knew a lot more than he did, judging by his crummy grades. He'd rattled them off the other day almost proudly, but they were nothing compared to her straight A's. "Just what wouldn't I know about?" she said.

"Your grandparents, for one."

Cass strained to see his face, his exact expression, but he was eyeing the ground. "What about my grandparents?"

"They've loved you all along, that's what."

"Right." Cass chuckled. "Tell me another one."

"I'm serious. Your grandpa showed me something that proved it. Told me to keep it a secret. Not that I *would.*"

Cass bit her lip and winced. "Well," she said, "I'm waiting."

"I can't *tell* you. You've got to see it with your own eyes."

"Fine. Then show me."

Jordy did not reply. He shook his head as if momentarily dazed. "Uh, whatever. But first I've got to get an orange."

Cass frowned but said nothing. She followed him along the levee until they came to an overpass, then crossed to the other side of the canal. Jordy ran down the embankment and disappeared into the trees. Cass shivered in the darkness. She wondered whether they were trespassing, whether there were armed guards patroling the groves for orange thieves. What was taking Jordy so long?

She squinted down row after row, trying to make out his form, but the denim jacket had been swallowed by the night. "Jordy?" she called softly. "Jordy, where are you?"

Gravel crunched behind her. She spun about to see him sneaking along the levee. "Come on," he whispered. "We've got to get out of here." Grabbing her hand and hunching forward, he dragged her toward the trailer park. Oranges dropped from his pockets and from the half-zipped front of his jacket, leaving a trail in their wake. Cass's side was aching by the time the trees gave way to new housing.

Jordy plopped to the ground. His hands were shaking as he tore the peel off an orange. Instead of offering Cass a section, he stuffed several in his mouth and chewed hungrily.

Cass lowered herself down beside him, watching him eat. "That's okay," she said at last. "I didn't want any."

Jordy banged his forehead with the heel of his hand. "I'm sorry. Here." He pulled another orange out of his sleeve. "Want it?"

Cass shook her head. He was acting like a guy possessed. "Are you okay?" she said. "What are you, an orange freak?"

Jordy laughed. "Hardly. I just needed a little sugar is all. I guess we walked farther than I thought."

"Sugar, you say?" Cass reached into her pocket and pulled out a roll of peppermint Life Savers. "Ask and you shall receive."

"That's okay," Jordy said. "I'll be all right in a few minutes."

First a shot, now sugar. He sounded just like that new kid who'd moved to her neighborhood in Iowa City from St. Paul. It was no secret that he had to go to the nurse's office for a shot every day before lunch. But one afternoon around Thanksgiving he'd been playing floor hockey and started staggering around, acting like he was drunk. Everyone had teased him, until the gym teacher went over with a little packet of something sweet and explained that the guy was having an insulin reaction, that his blood sugar was too low. Now Cass thought of Jordy's strange behavior and fitted together the pieces. "You're diabetic, aren't you?"

Jordy flicked his peels into the canal, one by one, not looking at her.

"It's stupid not to tell me," she said. "You know that, don't you?"

"Yeah, so? What's it to you?"

Cass struggled to her feet, dusting off her bottom. He could have had a reaction, could have fainted dead away and she wouldn't have even known how to help him. The fool. Anger rose in her cheeks, rebuffing the cool night air. "You sure know how to treat your friends, you know that? For your information, it's *nothing* to me, okay? Nothing!"

She turned toward the trailer park and took off running. The sound of gravel crunching beneath her feet spurred her on. A cloud skittered across the thready moon, making the sky and dark canal indistinguishable. She could feel her childhood panic setting in. But there were lights up ahead. If she kept going, she would be all right.

"Cass!" Jordy called. "Come back here!"

She didn't stop. Talk about grown-ups keeping secrets, she thought. What was *he* doing? How did he expect her to be his friend if he couldn't be honest about something as important as his diabetes?

The maze of trailers, confusing in their sameness, loomed before her. She glanced over her shoulder, but Jordy was not coming to bail her out. She was on her own. Maybe it was just as well. For all practical purposes, she'd been on her own for years—planning her meals, fixing up the flat, putting herself to bed when Mom was out late. At least there were still several porch lights on; she needn't face total darkness alone. All she had to do was find the social hall and backtrack to D Street. Alta Mesa might be huge, but if she kept her wits about her, she would be okay.

She stole across the field, her breath coming hard. Distant carols floated from the auditorium, guiding her way. Cass tried to imagine not seeing Jordy for the rest of her vacation. With or without him, she thought, I'll be all right. So why do I feel like crying?

Chapter 8

Jordy stared out the window at the McFerrens' trailer, trying to catch a glimpse of Cass. Surely she was there by now. He'd already tried the social hall, thinking that she would have stopped for punch and cookies after the pageant. And she hadn't been anywhere along the levee. Where else could she be but home? He could have kicked himself for not having given her a straight answer about his diabetes. She was right; it shouldn't be such a big deal.

Rusty padded into the living room and nuzzled Jordy's arm. "Gotta go out, boy?" he said. The red setter wagged his tail and pranced to the door. "All right. All right already, let me get my coat."

As he and the dog headed toward the rocky patch at the end of the street, Jordy's pulse quickened.

Someone was already down there. Could it be Cass? He broke into a jog. Rusty strained at the end of the leash.

"Hey!" he called.

The person turned, revealing a white poodle in her arms. Jordy's hopes fell as he realized it was an older woman, not Cass, bundled in a parka. "Good heavens!" she said. "You scared the breath right out of me."

"Sorry," he muttered. "I thought you were somebody else." He stroked Rusty's back absently. "Hurry up, boy. Do your thing."

Rusty obliged, and on the way back to the trailer, Jordy slowed in front of the McFerrens' and peeked in the window. One light burned over the kitchen sink, where someone was hunched over, either throwing up or eating something messy. Jordy let Rusty into his grandparents' trailer, then returned to the McFerrens', knocking lightly at the door. The landing trembled; someone was coming. Moments later, Cass appeared in the doorway, her face flushed, her hair disheveled.

"What do *you* want?" she said.

"I was worried about you. Are you okay?"

"Sure. Why wouldn't I be?" Cass stepped aside, but did not invite him in. "What about you? You okay?"

Jordy eyed his unlaced hightops. "You mean

. . . my reaction, right?" When he looked up, Cass's expression softened and she motioned him in. "Thanks."

"My grandparents are sleeping," she said, turning on a small table lamp. "We'll have to be quiet."

Jordy touched the gray metal file cabinet by the TV, hesitating to take a seat. "You're sure they're asleep?" he asked.

"I think so. Why?" Cass flopped down on the sofa, clasping a throw pillow to her chest. "Just what are you up to now?"

Jordy studied her face in the dim lamplight. Her eyes were puffy and kind of glazed-looking. Had she been crying? "I . . . I want to apologize," he said, "about before. You're right about the diabetes. I'm a Type I—you know, the kind that needs insulin shots. And if I forget to take them or I eat too much sugar, well, let's just say it could be diabetic coma time. But then again, if I take them and don't eat enough or exercise too much, you've got your exciting insulin reaction . . . like tonight. Fun stuff, huh?"

"Not really. This is serious. I wish you'd quit joking around."

"Okay, sorry," Jordy said, sobering. "Don't ask me why I didn't want you to know."

Cass chewed at her lip. "Why?" she said at last.

"Why what?"

"Why shouldn't I ask?"

Jordy blew out a long breath. "Because I don't know the answer, that's why."

"Bull," Cass said. "You do so. You're ashamed. You think it makes you somehow less than the rest of us."

"Don't tell me what I think. I hate that. You're not inside my head." But she was right, and he hated that even more.

"Fine. Think what you want." Cass tossed her head. "Anyway, it's good you told me. I mean, I'm glad you did."

"I'll bet you are," Jordy mumbled. Now he'd have *her* playing nursemaid, too. It wasn't enough to have Nana and Grandpa measuring every bite he ate, every mile he walked. "Look," he said, "I didn't come over here to fight."

"Thank goodness for small favors," Cass said.

Jordy sighed and urged himself to get on with it. Once she knew the truth about her grandparents, she'd have to talk to them about the departure date problem. No way she'd risk having them evicted, once she knew they really did love her.

"So," Cass said, "what *did* you come over here for?"

"To show you something, remember? I told you before. On the levee." Jordy opened the filing cabinet and withdrew the rubber-banded letters, placing them in her hand.

"What's all this?"

"Just look at 'em," Jordy said. "See for yourself."

As Cass flipped slowly through the pile, her eyebrows met in the middle. "I don't get it. . . ."

"Look at the postmarks," Jordy said.

"They go back *years.*" She pulled a gaily colored card out of one envelope and read it aloud. " 'Today you're five and we're so glad. You're the best granddaughter we've ever had.' " Her eyes teared up and she wiped them with a wadded tissue from her pocket. "Five," she said. "Can you believe it?"

Just then Muffin scratched on the bedroom door. Jordy scooped the letters up, stashing them quickly in the drawer. "I wasn't supposed to tell you about this," he said, "so keep it to yourself."

"But why are they all *here*? I don't get it."

"You mean you don't know who wrote 'return to sender'? Look again." With a glance at the closed bedroom door, Jordy retrieved the pile, flashing the top letter before her eyes. "Look familiar?"

Cass wrinkled her face up. "My mom makes her *E*'s like that but why would she . . ." Her voice trailed off and she raked her teeth over her chapped bottom lip. Jordy squirmed in the ensuing silence.

What have I done? he thought. I was only trying to help. He wondered whether he'd gone and spoiled things between Cass and her mother, just as

Mr. McFerren had feared. He wouldn't blame her a bit if she told him where to get off. He had no business sticking his nose where it didn't belong.

Cass rose and strode to the kitchen, her teeth beginning to chatter. She rubbed her arms briskly, scanning the darkened hallway for something without success. "Don't they have a thermostat in this place?" she said at last.

Jordy grabbed the afghan off the sofa back and draped it around her shoulders. "Better?"

Cass nodded. "My mom's not a monster, you know. She really isn't. She's irresponsible, yeah. But not mean. Why would she do it? I-I don't understand." She looked up at Jordy, her eyes brimming with confusion and pain.

Jordy shrugged, wished he could throw her some small scrap of reassurance.

"Maybe . . . I don't know . . . maybe she was afraid they'd spoil me or something. Dumb, right?"

Jordy shrugged. How could *he* say? He didn't know her mother at all.

"Do you think . . . oh, I don't know . . . that maybe she was afraid of losing me?"

"Losing you?" Jordy said.

"To them. You know." She was pacing the kitchen now, talking more to herself than to Jordy. "Yeah, maybe she was just so scared and alone. Like she wasn't in her right mind. That's probably it." She reached out, touched his arm. "Don't you think so?"

"Yeah," he said, tamping down the thought that her mom was more likely a spiteful witch. "I'm sure that's it."

Cass sighed, easing herself into her grandfather's recliner. "At least I know they *tried* to know me," she said. The possibility of a smile played on her lips. "I'm glad you showed me. Really, I am."

Jordy shifted his weight, feeling suddenly awkward. Maybe he should just go. Let her absorb all this tonight and press the point about the leaving thing in the morning when she was fresh. But it'll be Christmas, he thought. She'll be too busy. He cleared his throat, glancing nervously at the bedroom door. Muffin was definitely awake, and it wouldn't be long before the McFerrens were, too.

"The letters are our little secret, right?" he said.

Cass nodded, and he mustered his courage to push her further. "And you *are* going to tell your grandparents about that little problem you have, right?"

"What little problem?"

"Your eviction, remember? Come on, Cass. Nana says the manager's dead serious. You can't keep pretending it's nothing."

"Pardon me," Cass said, "but don't you think the whole thing's a bunch of crap?"

Jordy blinked at her directness, a huge grin erupting unbidden. "I couldn't have put it better myself. So," he said, tossing back his hair, "are we going to take this lying down or what?"

"I don't know. What can we do about it? We've done everything we can."

Jordy bit his knuckle, mulling possibilities over in his mind. A lot of people's rights were being violated here; he didn't need Dad around to tell him that. The situation called for action—a protest of some kind, or at the very least a petition. Dad didn't think twice about doing stuff like that in the sixties, and Jordy admired him for taking a stand. Sometimes you had to fight trouble with more trouble, he thought. But good would come of it. You just had to believe.

"I think we should organize," he said at last. "There's greater strength in numbers, you know."

Cass let the recliner snap upright and shrugged the afghan off her shoulders. "Numbers? There's only two of us. What can a couple of kids do, anyway? It's the residents who have to get up in arms, and from what you tell me, a lot of them would be only too glad to get rid of *all* of us kids."

Jordy thought of the big-mouthed walker. "Yeah," he said, "you're right about that."

Cass drew her teeth over her bottom lip. Creative wheels were obviously turning behind those bright blue eyes. At last she snapped her fingers. "I've got it! What we need are sponsors—someone with some influence around here."

"Don't look at me," Jordy said.

"Not *you,* dummy," she said. "Your grandparents. They know everybody. We'll write up a letter of protest and have them get signatures. Then the management will *have* to listen, don't you think?"

Jordy considered her scheme. "It's worth a shot," he said, though secretly he worried whether Nana and Grandpa would cooperate. Great risk takers they were not.

Cass got up and scrounged through a drawer in the kitchen for some paper and a pen. "Here," she said. "You write it."

The vinyl-covered dinette chair whispered as Jordy sat down. She leaned over his shoulder, standing so close that the scent of flowers sprang from her skin or from her hair. He couldn't tell which, and he was afraid to turn toward her to find out, lest his flushed cheeks give him away. His heart was racing, driving the right words from his mind. Chill out, man. Don't be a walking bag of hormones, he chided himself. She's just a *friend.*

"Well," she whispered, "what are you waiting for?"

Jordy shrugged. At least Muffin had settled down. He touched his earring, grounding himself in reality. Get to work. Stop goofing around. After all the petitions he'd written at school—most recently, one protesting the segregation of bag-lunch eaters and hot-lunch eaters—he figured stock phrases would flow effortlessly from his pen. But his mind was a blank.

"Oh, what's the use?" Cass said, taking the chair next to him. "It won't work. I just know it. Who's going to care about the rights of a couple of kids?"

Jordy chewed on the end of the pen, ignoring her comment. If he thought the way *she* did, Queen Anne Junior High would still be in the Dark Ages. Sure, his protests had raised eyebrows as well as issues. But it had been worth it to prove that change was not impossible. He saw no reason for things to be different here in Arizona. "We'll make them care," he said.

Cass touched his arm. "Jordy, just forget it. There's no way we're going to change anything."

"Bull." He scolded her with a look. "We can do anything we set our minds to. Anything."

Cass rolled her eyes. "Right. Tell me another one."

"I'm serious," Jordy said. "The problem with you is you have no guts."

Cass eyed her stomach ruefully. "Right," she said again. "Tell me another one."

Jordy sighed, combing his fingers through his

hair. Why did she have to go and turn everything he said around? It was so exasperating. "Would you just quit thinking about your weight all the time?" he said. "Big deal. So you have a few pounds to lose. Nobody's perfect."

Cass avoided his eyes. Her bottom lip was trembling. A knot rose in Jordy's throat and he swallowed hard. I've really put my foot in it this time, he thought. Now what do I do?

"Look, I'm sorry." He extended his long arms awkwardly. "Come here."

A small, choking sound escaped her lips as she leaned toward him, inclining her head. Her hair veiled her face. His hands connected with her shoulders, easing her closer, into his arms. He felt the sobs rising up inside her and patted her back, helpless to ease her pain.

"It's okay," Jordy said. "Let her rip."

Cass lifted her head off his shoulder, laughing through her tears. "You're too much, you know that?"

"Right," Jordy teased. "Tell me another one." He hugged her tighter, stroking her hair, until her back no longer jerked and twitched, until her breathing matched his.

Chapter 9

Cass fingered the folded edges of the petition in her pocket, reassuring herself that she hadn't forgotten it, that she and Jordy were doing the right thing. The line for Monday-night bingo inched forward and Grandfather waved three ten-dollar bills and three singles at the man behind the table. Where's Jordy? she wondered. He had promised he'd bring Hi and Dottie.

The man accepted the money and handed Grandma two stacks of bingo cards wrapped in newsprint sheets—a real bargain, he said, at fifteen dollars per packet—plus three green-edged admission cards. A cross-stitched bag bearing the likeness of a winning bingo swung from her forearm. Grandma examined one of the green cards and handed it back. "Give me the third one down," she said. "Threes are always lucky."

Cass swallowed her disbelief when the man obliged matter-of-factly, and followed her grandparents into the social hall. The rows of chairs from the Christmas pageant had been replaced by long tables. A lighted board and a contraption resembling a see-through vacuum cleaner with bouncing, numbered balls dominated the stage.

"Oh, Ed," Grandma said, "would you look at that? Someone's in my lucky chair."

Grandfather pressed his lips together, shook his head. "You'll find another, dear. Trust me."

Cass quickly scanned the seated players but there was no sign of Jordy or the Ginsburgs. Grandma finally settled on the third chair from the front, at the third table from the door. Cass rolled her eyes. Unbelievable.

Once seated, her grandmother emptied the contents of her bag onto the table: three colored ink-dabbers, a plastic sheet, a roll of Scotch tape, a magnetic wand, a small box of round, metal-edged plastic chips, and a tiny ceramic penguin.

"What's this for?" Cass said, fingering the black-and-white figurine.

"Why, luck, of course." Grandma whisked it out of Cass's hands and placed it in the middle of her green admission card's *O.* "There," she said, arranging the last of her thirty-four red-edged cards in a grid that extended from her to Cass. "All set. I'm counting on you to help me now, Cass." She glanced at her watch. "They're late. Again."

Grandfather patted her arm. "Calm down now. You're going to get your blood pressure up."

Cass trained her eyes on the doorway. Not only residents but younger people—women mostly, some with infants in carriers—began to stream in. At last Jordy rushed toward her, carrying a single green-edged card. He slapped it upside down on the table.

"Where *are* they?" Cass said, her voice hushed. "I thought you said—"

"They won't come." Jordy was fuming; she could practically see his pulse pounding in his temples when he flipped back his hair. He looked around, lowered his voice. "Said they wouldn't be caught dead at a bingo game. No offense."

"But did you explain about the petition?" It's not going to work, she thought. What did I tell you?

"I tried to, but they had some phony baloney excuse why they couldn't sign it. Something about how would it look, them being on the staff and all." Jordy folded himself into the chair beside her. "Forget 'em," he said. "We can do it *without* their help."

"You really think so?"

"Absolutely!"

She wished she could share his conviction. "Here it is," she said, pulling the petition from her pocket. "I like the way you worded it. Especially that part about discrimination on the basis of age. That ought to get them, don't you think? Especially these old people."

"I hope so." Jordy pulled out a pen. "Maybe we'd better start now, before the game begins." He glanced at the paper. "Hey! Your grandparents didn't sign it."

Cass embraced herself as if to contain the hammering in her chest. How could she tell him that she hadn't even bucked up the courage to tell them about the *problem,* let alone to ask for their signatures? What if the news made Grandma's blood pressure go up? What if she had a stroke? No, there was no sense worrying them until she had to. And with Jordy running the show, she was betting she wouldn't have to at all.

"Don't bother them about it now," she said. "Grandma's really into this bingo stuff. She says writing before a game will spoil her luck."

"Give me a break."

Cass shrugged. It was the best excuse she could think of. And considering the way Grandma was acting, Cass probably wasn't far from the truth.

"Okay, fine," Jordy said. "Let's go make the rounds and leave *them* for later."

Jordy's chair scritched across the parquet floor. Cass rose to join him, but Grandma caught her arm. "Where are you going, honey? I need you here for good luck."

Cass shrugged helplessly at Jordy.

"We're taking around the—"

"Survey," Cass blurted, turning toward her grandparents. She hoped her body would block Jordy from their view. There was no way she wanted them seeing the way his mouth was hanging open in surprise. "But he can do it without me, right, Jordy?"

He scowled as she shot him a pointed look. "Cass," he hissed.

She let her eyes plead her case.

"Later for you," he said. Skulking off toward the first table, he began working the bingo crowd for signatures. Thank goodness for Jordy, she thought with a sigh of relief. What would I do without him?

The bingo caller seated himself behind the bouncing-ball machine and announced the first game—single bingo, any direction, including the inside and outside four corners. Grandma swept up a handful of chips, urging Cass to do the same. "I'm not as quick as I used to be," she confessed. "Maybe you can help me out. Not that we keep our winnings, honey. Ed and I like giving it to charity, you understand. But it's fun just the same."

Grandfather pulled a rolled news magazine out of his back pocket and disappeared between its covers. Grandma would get no help from him, Cass realized, and gathered some chips of her own.

As the caller droned out the numbers, Cass fidgeted in her chair. How's Jordy doing? she wondered. Is he having any luck? She glanced over her shoulder in time to see a petite Hispanic woman flick him away as if he were a mosquito. The woman had obviously missed hearing the last number and appeared peeved to have to ask her neighbor what it was.

Jordy made a face and an obscene gesture behind the woman's back, and grudgingly folded the petition up. Now he looked like a human thundercloud rolling Cass's way. She braced herself for the storm.

"Great. This is just great," he muttered, making no effort to keep his voice down. He slapped the petition on the table in front of Cass, right on top of some of her grandmother's bingo cards.

"Jor-dy!"

"Sh!" Grandma hissed. She plucked the offending paper from the table and set it down by Grandfather.

Cass's heart was doing double-time. She couldn't very well get up and grab the petition without attracting more attention from her grandparents than she wanted. But if she left the paper there, one of them was bound to read it, and *then* what would she do?

"Five signatures," Jordy said. "That's all I got. Look at that thing. We're just going to have to hustle between games."

Cass nodded numbly. Someone yelled "Bingo!" and the room dissolved into disgruntled rumblings and the metallic clicking of wands collecting chips from the game cards.

"You want me to answer your survey questions?" Grandma said, picking up the petition. "Give me a pen."

Cass's breath caught in her throat as she watched her grandmother read the paper. Grandma's eyebrows knit together and the color drained from her face.

"Cassie, what's this all about?" she said. "I don't understand." Her hand massaged the flat expanse above her fallen bosom. "I thought school didn't start until after the sixth."

"It doesn't," Cass managed. Her voice sounded raspy, unreal.

"You never even told them, did you?" Jordy said.

He tugged on her arm, and she felt caught between the two of them.

"Does this mean you can't stay until the sixth?" Grandma said. "I mean, you're not *allowed* to?"

Cass nodded, and Jordy chimed in, "Supposedly you'll get evicted if she does."

"But how can this be? We *live* here. You're our guest. They can't tell us we have to kick you out. Ed!" She elbowed her husband out from behind his magazine. "Will you look at what they're trying to do to us?"

She passed Grandfather the petition and he read it quickly. Deep wrinkles creased his forehead. "No one's kicking our grandbaby out without a fight, Leah." He nodded at Jordy. "Give me that pen, son."

"You mean it?" Cass said, excitement buoying her out of her chair.

Her grandparents nodded in unison.

"Far out!" Jordy said.

Grandfather scrawled his name, then passed the petition to his wife. The bingo caller was asking everyone to get ready for the second game—a plus sign.

"What else can we do to help?" Grandfather asked. "Just say the word."

Jordy eyed the microphone on stage. "Think you can get him to let us ask for signatures?" he said.

Cass's stomach felt all fluttery. Things were rolling. And Grandma was taking the bad news in stride. At least *her* grandparents were going along with the petition. That was a surprise. Maybe they were a lot more gutsy than they seemed. And maybe once the McFerrens talked to Hi and Dottie, Jordy's grandparents would come around, too.

Grandfather was making his way stiffly toward the stage, and the bingo caller came forward to see what he wanted. Moments later, Grandfather motioned for Cass to come up and use the mike.

She shook her head, her heart beating fast, and nudged Jordy out of his chair. "You do it," she said. "I hate getting up in front of people."

"I'll talk," he said, "but you've gotta come with me, at least."

Cass blew out a long breath. "All right. Let's get it over with."

As Jordy explained Cass's predicament to the packed crowd, she cringed under the staring gaze of hundreds of eyes. What are these people thinking? she wondered. That we're troublemakers?

"We don't want to mess up your game or anything like that," Jordy said. "But if you could just sign this when it comes around, it would really help a lot, okay?"

He hopped off the stage while Cass lingered to thank the bingo caller. When her voice echoed through the sound system, she felt hot enough to melt right through the floor.

During the next two games the petition seemed to fly throughout the room, and when Jordy finally reclaimed it, about a hundred signatures blackened both sides. Slapping it on the table before Cass, he punched the air in triumph.

"We did it!" he said. "Now they'll *have* to change the rule."

Grandfather and Grandma exchanged a look that Cass did not understand. "It's a start, anyway," Grandma said. "We'll give you that."

"*Now* what do we do?" Cass said.

"Take it to the manager. What else?" Jordy folded the petition in half. "Come on."

"Right now?" Grandma asked. "Can't it wait till after bingo? Never know *when* we might get a run of good luck."

Jordy shrugged, and Cass said, "Yeah, Jordy, you never know." She was thinking about how well things had gone for them that night. Who knew what could happen next?

Jordy winked at her. "Yeah, Cass," he said, laughter dancing in his hazel eyes. "Never know when we'll get a run of good luck."

Color rose in her cheeks. Her mind flipped back to the way he'd hugged her on Christmas Eve and to the mistletoe he'd noticed and apologized about earlier the same night. What good luck was he talking about? The petition . . . or their having met?

Chapter 10

When Jordy opened his eyes the next morning, the first thing on his mind was the petition. What was the manager going to do about it? When he and Cass had stopped by his trailer the night before to give it to him, he had been polite but noncommittal. At least he had heard them out. We've got a shot, Jordy thought. It's not over yet.

Sunlight streamed through a crack in the drapes behind his sofa bed, illuminating the darkened hallway. The telephone rang, and Nana rushed out of the bedroom, her satiny nightgown skimming her body. She grabbed the receiver in mid-ring, stretching the curly cord to its limit as she backed toward her room.

Jordy strained to hear whether it was Cass. Maybe

she had news. But from the way Nana was shooting angry looks his way, he figured it had to be Mom. I've been gone for over a week, he thought. How could she possibly have found something to pin on me? He scanned his memory, trying to dig up an as-yet-undiscovered prank that he might have pulled on Becca or Amy before he left, but came up empty. Heck, he hadn't even made off with their creme rinse as he had done the summer before, when he went to camp. No, there was nothing to feel guilty about. Flipping the covers aside, he pulled his jeans on, bare feet slapping across the vinyl as he strode toward Nana.

"*Now* what'd I do?" he said. "Let me talk to her."

Nana waved him away, her lips pressed into a tight line. Jordy's heartbeat thrummed in his ears as he waited. Surely Mom would want to talk to him. Why wouldn't Nana at least let him defend himself?

"Give it to me," he said. "Let me talk to her."

Nana snapped her fingers and glowered at him. "Yes, *Mr. Cotter*," she said pointedly. "We'll be there at eight-thirty. All three of us."

Mr. Cotter. The manager. Jordy swallowed hard. Things did not sound good. He wondered whether Cass had gotten a call, too.

As Nana cradled the receiver, she spun on him, her eyes flashing. "Didn't we tell you to stay out of trouble?" she said. "Don't you realize what you've done?"

"No," Jordy said. "What?" Here it comes, he thought. Brace yourself.

"You've ruined our reputation around here. But that doesn't mean anything to *you,* does it? No. All you ever think about is yourself."

Jordy licked his lips, pressed them together. Not true. She's lying. Just tune her out.

"Jordan, I'm talking to you. The manager is fit to be tied about that little petition you and Cass dropped off last night. Do you hear me?"

How can I help it? You're screaming in my ear. Jordy blinked at her, retaining his cool. "If he's upset, it's because he knows he's wrong," Jordy said. "I hope the media get hold of this. He doesn't have a case and he knows it."

"My grandson, the lawyer," Nana said, throwing her hands up. "And the media better *not* get hold of this, young man."

Jordy smiled on the inside. The media! Why didn't we think of that before? Cass is sure to hate the attention, but it might be our only chance to shame Mr. Cotter into letting her stay till the sixth. He wondered when he could break away to tell her his new plan.

"He wants to see us in an hour," Nana said, "so you'd better hurry up and do your thing."

Why didn't she just say "test your blood" or "take your insulin"? Maybe if we don't talk about it, Jordy thought, my diabetes will go away, right? Wrong! He'd been wishing it would ever since it was diagnosed eighteen months before. He'd even tried making deals with God: "I'll never talk back to anyone if You *please* make it go away. I promise, God, no more trouble—ever—if You just let me off the hook with this one thing. I'll never ask You for anything again as long as I live." God had to be deaf, Jordy figured, because no hearing being would have turned him down on such an offer.

Now he could hear Nana in the back bedroom, recounting Mr. Cotter's complaints to Grandpa. Jordy ducked into the bathroom and ran the water. Somehow he had to call some reporters. It was their only hope. Then he and Cass would cut out for the day and let Mr. Cotter take the heat. Of course, they'd play the innocents to the hilt on their return, but the story would be out. There'd be no way to stop it. And if Mr. Cotter *still* didn't let Cass stay, maybe one of those ACLU guys would take her case. They were bound to have an office in Phoenix. And if worse came to worst, he could always call Dad. "Brilliant, Sondel," Jordy praised himself. "You've got it licked."

Jordy gave himself his shot and gulped down his breakfast, ignoring his grandparents' silence and pained expressions. Then he excused himself, saying he'd left something over at Cass's.

"Hurry back," Grandpa said. "We don't want to keep Mr. Cotter waiting now, do we?" Sarcasm clung to each word. Jordy scowled. He's treating me like some dumb kid, he thought.

At the McFerrens' trailer, he tapped on the window above Cass's sofa sleeper. Moments later her face parted the curtains and she opened the window an inch. "What's going on?" she asked, her voice still husky with sleep.

Jordy quickly filled her in on Mr. Cotter's call. "Just let me in. Quick," he said. "I've got to make a couple calls."

She appeared in the doorway moments later, swathed in an afghan. "If I'd known you were coming, I'd have worn my good quilt," she teased.

Jordy smiled. She's definitely no Jennifer, he thought. If she were, she'd never have let him see her without makeup, let alone the perfect outfit. And a true Jennifer would never joke about being seen as she really was first thing in the morning.

"What are *you* grinning at?" Cass said, stepping aside to allow him entry.

"Nothing."

"Bull." She hugged the afghan tighter. "You're laughing at me, aren't you?"

"Really, I'm not."

"Then tell me."

"I was just thinking how different you are . . ." Different. Wrong word. Try again. Quick. "Better, I mean, than most girls."

Cass's mouth twitched from side to side. Somehow his compliment wasn't getting through.

"What I mean is, you're not a Jennifer." Cass frowned and he blundered on. "You know, not a phony. You're—how to put it—*real.*"

"Thank you, I think." A smile creased her cheeks as she pointed out the telephone and pulled the yellow directory from a drawer.

Muffin started scratching on the bedroom door. Jordy froze, afraid the noise would wake Cass's grandparents.

"Don't worry," Cass said. "Grandma has an early doctor's appointment, so she'll be getting up anyway."

"Good." Jordy's fingers walked through the TV station listings. "I won't be long, but stall my grandparents if they come looking for me, okay?"

After leaving detailed messages with one secretary and two news hotline answering machines, he called the local newspaper and talked with the city desk editor.

"Let me get this right," the guy said. "You two kids are taking the trailer park to court?"

Jordy swallowed quickly. He didn't want to lie.

But he couldn't tell whether the editor was taking him seriously. If not, the guy would never send a reporter. Jordy cleared his throat. "We're going to do whatever it takes," he said. "Maybe even involve the ACLU." *That* would get him.

"Well, I'm not promising anything. Depends what kind of a news day we have. But maybe I'll be able to spring somebody to go over and check it out. What'd you say your name was?"

Jordy's thoughts raced. He'd wanted to keep his name out of this, to let Mr. Cotter take the heat. It wasn't like he wanted the newspaper to do a feature article on him and Cass—two gutsy kids fighting the system, that'd be their angle. On the other hand, he wasn't ashamed of his involvement. And if he and Cass were off at a movie or someplace when the reporter came, Mr. Cotter would still be on the line.

"You there?" the editor said.

"Yes, sir." Jordy steeled his resolve. "My name's Jordy. Jordan, really. Sondel. And my friend is Cass McFerren."

After he hung up, he said to Cass, "Keep the day free, okay? Things may heat up around here and we'd better be gone when they do."

"Fine," Cass said. "Keep me posted and I'll catch you later."

As Jordy and his grandparents walked to the manager's office in the main building, he fondled the knowledge of his secret media contact as if it were a forbidden pet hidden deep in his pocket. Mr. Cotter can't touch me, he thought. I'm within my rights. He noticed that Grandpa's profile was set in marble, while Nana kept shooting worried glances her husband's way. Could Mr. Cotter touch *them*? That was guilt by association, wasn't it? Nana said Jordy only cared about himself, but that wasn't true. He didn't want them to get caught in the cross fire; he only wanted what was right.

Mr. Cotter ushered them into his paneled office and closed the door. His half glasses were perched on the tip of his bulbous, sunburned nose. "Take a seat," he said, though there were only two chairs besides his.

"I'll stand," Jordy said, needlessly because everyone else obviously expected him to.

Mr. Cotter leveled him with an icy-blue stare. Let him talk. You didn't do anything wrong, Jordy reminded himself. It's *his* problem, not yours.

"Dottie, Hi, we just can't have this kind of thing." Mr. Cotter pushed the petition toward them. "It looks bad, the grandson of staff running us down like that, don't you think?"

Dottie fidgeted with her wedding ring but said nothing.

"Hi, how 'bout you? You *must* see my point on this. We've got folks calling every day, hoping we have space for them—all because we run a clean park, a quiet park. And you can't do that with kids running around all the time. Not that I've got anything against kids. But what are folks gonna think if I give in to this kind of nonsense? That they can walk all over me, that's what. And then where will we be?"

Grandpa cleared his throat. Jordy swallowed hard, trying to anticipate the words. He's a troublemaker, always has been. His mother can't handle him and neither can we. Grandpa looked from Nana to Jordy, then leveled his gaze at Mr. Cotter. "He's really not a bad kid, Hecky. Just trying to do right by his friend is all."

Jordy blinked in disbelief. Grandpa defending him? Was Jordy hallucinating?

Mr. Cotter blew his nose into a plaid handkerchief, then stuffed it back in his pocket. "So I'm to understand you're taking his side in this?"

Nana licked her lips quickly, her eyes flitting from Mr. Cotter to Grandpa and back. "It's not that. It's just—"

"Yes," Grandpa said. "I guess I am." He seemed as surprised as everyone else to hear how emphatically the words flew from his mouth. "I may not like his methods, Hecky, but I sure do respect his right to fight for what he believes. I guess he's like his father that way."

At the comparison to Dad, a satisfying warmth crept into Jordy's cheeks. He clenched a fist at his side, felt like shoving it high in the air. Yeah, Grandpa! Way to be!

Nana's nostrils flared with frustration. She nudged Grandpa but he refused to acknowledge her as he continued. "Don't get me wrong. Dottie and I, we like it here at Alta Mesa. We like teaching, like the people. And we hope you'll keep us on. But I won't sell out my own grandson in order to stay. That I won't do."

Jordy's heart hammered against his rib cage. Grandpa *was* defending him. He'd just put everything on the line, in fact. Jordy'd heard more than he'd ever dreamed possible. Whatever Mr. Cotter said now didn't matter. Grandpa *believed* in him. And if that didn't restore Jordy's faith in the power of optimism, nothing would. No, he thought, there's just no point in always assuming the worst the way Cass does. Figuring that now he should make himself scarce, Jordy offered to wait in the lounge so the adults could talk.

Nana managed a brave little smile of thanks at his suggestion. She looked like a schoolgirl in the principal's office, awaiting her punishment. Somehow her feisty demeanor had dissolved, and when she mumbled, "What Grandpa said goes for me, too," her eyes held a silent apology.

Jordy closed the door tightly, surprised that he felt no desire to eavesdrop. Whatever they were saying had nothing to do with him. Not anymore. Now Nana and Grandpa had their own consequences to face, but ones they'd chosen. And that was what mattered. He paced in front of the bulletin board by the reception desk, scanning the index card ads listing items for sale—stained-glass sun catchers, a hide-a-bed, crocheted dishrags. A hand-lettered poster in the corner caught his eye.

Bike and Hike to the Wind Caves was printed in bold, black felt pen above a glossy photo of a red mountain and a small map detailing the route from Alta Mesa. *Check Out Bicycles at Reception. Free.*

Bingo! Jordy snapped his fingers. That's where we can go today, he thought. Cass is going to love it.

Chapter 11

Cass pedaled madly to keep up with Jordy. Her thighs were aching already, and her fingers had begun to cramp around the brown paper sack she clutched over the handlebar. Emblazoned in white on the mountain before them was the word *Phoenix* and an arrow pointing west. Desert stretched on either side of the roadway, spiked with giant saguaros. If she was ever going to write a travel feature about this place, she realized, she ought to take her time and make detailed mental notes. "Jordy," she hollered, "what's the big hurry? Slow down!"

Jordy obliged, and she pedaled up alongside him. "What'd you tell your grandparents?" he asked.

"Just that we were going on a bike ride. Why? What'd you tell yours?"

"Nothing."

"Nothing? Why not? Aren't they going to worry?"

Jordy threw back his head, let the wind divide and conquer his wild patch of bleached hair. He was wearing only a white T-shirt; she shivered inside her cut-off sweatshirt and windbreaker, waiting patiently for his reply. Why didn't he answer her?

"Jordy, I'm not kidding. Didn't you tell them anything?"

"They were already off teaching," he said. "I left a note."

There was more than the sun dancing in his eyes, and suspicion nipped at Cass's stomach. "A note, huh? What'd it say?"

"Oh, nothing much," he replied. Too casually.

"Yeah?" Cass said. "Define 'nothing much.' "

"I thanked them for supporting me, of course, but said we just couldn't hang around anymore, waiting for Mr. Cotter to take us seriously. That maybe now he'd see we meant business."

Cass braked to an abrupt halt. What did he think he was doing, leaving a message like that? Everyone was going to think they'd run away. "You're crazy, Jordy Sondel," she yelled after him. "Do you know that?"

Jordy circled back and dismounted. "What do you mean? All I said was—"

"Don't you see?" Cass sighed, flicked her hair back in frustration. "They're going to think we ran away!"

Jordy scoffed, but there was mischief in his eyes. "You really think so? Gee. But I was only talking about us calling the news media. Once that reporter starts nosing around, they'll know what I meant—that we just wanted to keep out of it."

Cass shook her head. Jordy was too smart to leave a confusing note like that. No, he knew exactly what effect his words would have. He *wanted* to make everyone worry. Probably figured that it would make better copy, arouse more sympathy. "Why didn't you just tell them we were going to the Wind Caves?" she said.

Jordy shrugged. "It says so on the checkout sheet in the office. Big deal. Come on. Stop being such a worry wart. We're almost there."

Grudgingly Cass remounted her bike and pedaled after him. Maybe he was right; she worried too much, always expected the worst. She ought to just kick back and let his optimism pull her along in its jet stream.

Before long Jordy turned off the main road and into a parking lot. Lavatories and a public phone peeked between a motor home and a dilapidated white Volkswagen. Jordy chained their bikes to the welcome sign at the foot of the trail while Cass examined the sack lunch she'd hastily thrown together. The apples hadn't squished the turkey sandwiches too badly, but the cinnamon cookies were now in crumbs. Oh well. Maybe Jordy wasn't even supposed to eat cookies. . . . How was *she* supposed to know?

Shading her eyes against the late morning sun, she surveyed the switchback trail that scarred the imposing red mountain. They hadn't even hit the path, let alone begun the climb to the Wind Caves, and already she wished they'd brought a canteen. Trying in vain to sweep the grit from her teeth with her tongue, she sneaked a butterscotch Life Saver from her pocket and rolled it around her mouth. If she expected to survive this desert outing, she'd have to guard these with her life.

"What are you waiting for?" Jordy said. "A helicopter?"

"Very funny." Cass hustled toward him, and they tramped on in silence until Jordy found a dead saguaro and removed two ribs, one of which he offered to Cass. "What's *that* for?" she said. "I look like I need a cane?"

"No, a walking stick," Jordy corrected. "Keeps you from sliding on the gravel."

"Oh." Cass took the stick, chagrined at her own defensiveness. Why couldn't she accept a simple kindness without seeing it as some kind of an insult?

What a pain she was! It was a wonder Jordy put up with her.

"So," Jordy said, "have you heard from your mom?"

Cass shook her head. Not that she'd expected to. Not that she was disappointed. What would she say to Mom anyway? How's your love life? And, by the way, why did you send Grandma and Grandfather's letters back?

Jordy nudged her arm, bringing her back to reality. "What? Sorry."

"It's okay. I said I haven't heard from my mom either, but that's *good* news. Who I'd really like to hear from is Dad."

Cass nodded sympathetically. A divorced father was better than a dead one, she figured, but not by much. At least her memories of Dad weren't clouded by bitterness and disappointment. In her fantasies, he was still her gallant prince on a Harley, and Mom (the beautiful Princess Kelly) still clung to his waist, her blond hair whipped by the wind.

"How'd your dad die, anyway?" Jordy said.

Cass blinked at him, the question colliding with her thoughts. "On a . . . in a . . . accident," she said, choking on the word *motorcycle.* "He wasn't wearing a helmet."

She felt Jordy's hand slip, warm, into hers. "Bummer," he said, his eyes trained on the trail ahead. "Sorry."

"Yeah. Me, too."

The sun inched higher in the sky. Cass hoped Jordy wouldn't notice the perspiration already beading under her bangs. He wasn't even breathing hard, but it was all Cass could do to keep from panting. The gravel trail narrowed as it cut back and forth across the lower slope of the mountain. Jordy let go of her hand. As they gained elevation, huge boulders rose on both sides, walling them in.

Cass eyed the rocks nervously. "Are there any rattlesnakes around here?"

"I doubt it."

"That's *not* what I wanted to hear. A simple *no* would have been . . ." Her voice trailed off. Had Jordy quickened his pace? She struggled to catch up, planting her walking stick firmly with each stride. "How 'bout we stop for lunch?" she said at last. "Aren't you hungry?"

Jordy shook his head. "Let's wait till we reach the caves. It'll be cool up there. I bet you can see for miles."

Cass sighed and tagged after him. Maybe he *wasn't* hungry, but shouldn't he eat something anyway, considering his diabetes and all? The problem was suggesting it without his blowing his stack. "I don't know about you," she said, "but I feel kind of shaky. Maybe we *should* eat. Share an apple or something."

Jordy kept walking, did not turn around. "Yeah, yeah, yeah. I hear you."

"So?"

"So get off my back."

Cass sighed and hurried after him. "Jordy! Don't be that way. I was only trying to help."

"You and the rest of the world." The trail angled more steeply upward. Jordy pressed on, his jaw set.

Cass's heart was pounding in her chest from the effort of the climb. She felt as if she were sucking air through a clogged straw. What was the elevation anyway? She glanced over her shoulder at the sprawl that was Mesa far below. What was Jordy doing, trying to break some kind of record? Why couldn't they stop and rest?

"Aren't you coming?" Jordy called down to her from a rocky ledge where the trail turned back on itself.

"I'm tired." She tried to keep the whine from her voice, and wondered whether she'd succeeded.

"We're not even halfway there yet. Just pace yourself."

"I'm trying but . . ." She hung her head. Shame warmed her cheeks. Jordy might have diabetes, she thought, but he's definitely a lot more fit than I am.

"Look, I *want* to go on. I do. But I just can't, Jordy, I really can't."

Jordy's shoulders raised and lowered in what appeared to Cass to be a great, disgusted sigh. "Try," he said.

Cass's lower lip trembled. Why was he so angry? You'd think she was spoiling his chance at placing in the Olympics or something. "Jordy, you're in shape," she blurted. "But what about me? Do I look like I'm cut out for Queen of the Bike-and-Hike?"

Jordy did not reply. He just stood there, fiddling with his stupid earring. "Are you saying you're giving up?" he asked at last.

Cass shrugged. "I just don't think I can make it without a rest. Maybe after lunch."

"Maybe tomorrow or the next day," Jordy said. "How do you know you can't make it if you don't even try?"

"I *am* trying. What do you think I've been doing for the last hour and a half? Heck, I was pooped after the bike ride."

"I know what you're up to and it's not going to work," Jordy said. "I'm going up to the caves—with or without you. So what's it gonna be?"

Cass drew in a long, steadying breath. She didn't know what he thought her angle was; all she knew was that she was too tired to take another step. He could hate her if he wanted to.

"Well?" Jordy said, his arms folded across his chest.

"I guess . . . I-I'll wait for you here." Cass scuffed the gravel with the toe of her sneaker. "Be careful, okay?"

"Right." His tone dripped with sarcasm.

"I mean it, Jordy. And . . . and I'm sorry."

"No skin off *my* nose. Be sorry for yourself. You're the one who's missing everything." He turned his back on her then, and she watched the bobbing white of his T-shirt until she could no longer see it against the chalky striations in the face of the mountain.

For a time she busied herself with the view. A blanket of haze hung over Phoenix. Trailer roofs below her in Mesa glinted in the sun. Nearby, teddy-bear cacti glistened like piles of light-green snowballs in the middle of the desert. An elderly couple, descending from the caves, stopped to ask if she was hurt. Soon after, two women about her mother's age came down, sliding and giggling and not even bothering to return Cass's greeting.

Out of boredom more than hunger, she finally ate her sandwich, then stretched out on a flat rock, her face turned to the sun. Clouds sauntered past like a parade of circus animals, and she closed her eyes. The desert sang a lullaby of birds on the updraft, whispers in the wind. Red and green geometrics swirled behind her eyelids, hypnotizing her, sucking her down . . . down . . . as she fell, heavy yet weightless, into a great abyss. . . .

"Jor-dy!" Had she screamed the words or only dreamed them? Cass bolted to her feet, squinting up at the mountain. The short, fat shadow she'd lain on earlier now pointed toward the Wind Caves like a gaunt stranger. Cupping her hands to her mouth, she screamed Jordy's name. It echoed off the face, unanswered.

Cass swallowed hard. Her heart shifted gears. Why wasn't he back yet? She checked her watch. It was late—almost four o'clock. Surely if he'd come down, he wouldn't have left her there, sleeping. She scanned the parking lot below—now deserted—and could just discern the frames of two bikes, propped against the sign. No, Jordy was still up there.

Panic slugged her in the stomach like a fist. Oh, no! she thought. He's had a reaction. He's lying up there somewhere, unconscious. Indecision rooted her to the spot. She was halfway between the telephone in the parking lot and Jordy, wherever he was. Maybe around the next turn in the trail. Or the next. She had to try to find him. He'd exercised too much, hadn't eaten enough. He would need sugar to prevent an insulin reaction, and she still had some Life Savers.

Grabbing up her staff and the sack lunch, she hit

the trail at a run. Adrenaline pounded through her veins, spurring her on. Just one more turn, she told herself again and again. It was a game, she realized, a trick she played to keep herself going. Soon her breath was coming in ragged gasps, but she pressed on.

It seemed to her as if Jordy had given up on her earlier. But maybe it was really Cass who'd given up on herself. Hadn't he been there for her all week, encouraging her, giving her moral support? Hadn't he told her that all she had to do was to keep trying?

She spied a patch of white above and to the right of her. Maybe it was Jordy! For an instant, she considered abandoning the snaking trail and carving her own path. But the mountain was too steep, the terrain too rugged. "Jordy!" she yelled. "Hold on! I'm coming!"

Her voice bounced back off the mountain. In her haste to reach him, she tripped over a rock, skinning her hands. Dabbing the blood on her jeans, she gingerly took up her walking stick and pressed on. The wind was beginning to whistle around her, or maybe it was coyotes gearing up for the night. Cass shivered. She swore at Jordy. What was he trying to prove?

At last she found him near the mouth of the Wind Caves, not quite unconscious, but very disoriented and pale. He was sitting in the middle of the trail, his head propped in his hands. When she touched his shoulder, he gazed up at her, confused.

"It's me, Cass," she said. Her fingers tore at the package of Life Savers. Thank God he hasn't passed out. It's not too late. "Here. Suck on this."

Jordy blindly obeyed, but his hand, his whole body, was trembling as he reached out to her. "I'm okay," he said without conviction.

"The heck you are. Can you stand?"

Jordy made a feeble attempt to rise but fell back again. A sob caught in his throat. "Shit," he whispered. "It's not fair. It's not frigging fair at all."

Cass knelt beside him, cradling his head against her breast, stroking his hair. "I know," she said. "I know." She held him for a long moment. But his trembling worsened. The Life Savers weren't helping! She had to get him to a hospital—quick.

Slipping off her windbreaker, she draped it around his shoulders. Then she unwrapped the last two candies and placed one in each of his hands. "Try to stay awake. Jordy? Do you hear me? I'm going to call for help."

He neither nodded nor blinked any indication that he'd heard her.

Cass bit her lip, cupped his face in her hands. "Hold on," she said fiercely. "Be strong. Help's coming."

Half running, half sliding down the mountain,

Cass figured even wings could not have helped her cover the distance faster. Racing the last several yards to the telephone, she fumbled breathlessly for a quarter. All she had was a wadded dollar bill. Tears welled up, but she fought them back. Be calm. Read the directions. Maybe emergency calls are free.

She faced the phone, took her own advice. Then she dialed 911, embracing the silvery metal machine as if it were her savior. When the dispatcher answered, Cass gave her location and explained Jordy's predicament. "He's diabetic," she said, "and he can't make it down from the mountain."

"We'll send an Airevac chopper," the woman said. "Don't worry. Are you all right?"

Cass nodded.

"I said—"

"Yes," Cass interrupted, realizing her failure to answer the question aloud. "I'm fine, really."

"Good." The woman's voice seemed to smile through the receiver. "You just make a collect call to your folks and stay put, okay?"

"Okay." Cass's voice sounded suddenly small, and she repeated herself to make sure the woman had heard. Then she dialed Operator and placed a collect call to her grandparents.

Grandfather answered on the first ring. "Thank the Lord it's you, Cassie. Are you okay? We've all been sick with worry. I thought you said you were going for a ride. Why did you two do a fool thing like run away?"

"We didn't, and I'm fine. It's Jordy," she said, as if that explained everything. "I already called Airevac and it's on the way. Can you get Hi and Dottie and drive out to the Wind Caves?"

"Sure thing, honey," he said. "They've been waiting by the phone, too. Now you stay right there, hear?"

"But what if the helicopter gets here first? I want to go with Jordy."

"I know," Grandfather said. "But we need you to tell us where they've taken him."

Cass sighed. She guessed that Phoenix had a lot more hospitals to choose from than Iowa City. "Okay."

"Atta girl. We'll meet up with Jordy at the hospital."

"Grandfather?"

"I'm still here."

"I-I'm sorry," Cass said. "Tell Grandma, too, will you? I didn't mean to make you worry."

"Promise you'll tell her yourself . . . later . . . at the hospital."

"I promise," Cass said. But as she hung up the phone, she wondered, Why tell her at the hospital? What's wrong with telling her in the car?

Chapter 12

What's that endless beeping? Jordy struggled to open his eyes. He felt as if any second his head would explode. What *is* that, anyway? Shades of blue swam into focus: icy walls, navy curtains. A metal IV pole towered over him, piping clear fluid into his arm from a suspended plastic bag.

"Jordy? Are you awake?"

He recognized Nana's voice immediately and strained to sit up. A cool hand eased him back, pulled the sheets about his chin. "Hush now. Relax. That's the way." She was leaning over him, and he swallowed hard, noticing how she seemed to have aged since that morning. He saw gray hairs among the blonde ones, and her wrinkles didn't look like laugh lines. "Gave us quite a scare, young man. Quite a scare."

Jordy nodded weakly. "Where's Grandpa?" he said.

"Down the hall with Cass."

Cass. He touched a tethered hand to his cheek, recalled the comforting feel of it against Cass's chest earlier on the mountain. Hold on. Help's coming. Be strong. Try to stay awake. Her words rebounded inside his head, making him wince. "Is she . . . what happened? I can't remember."

"Cass is fine. Just tired is all. Dozed off in the car on the way over," Nana said. "You should worry about yourself. Concentrate on getting well."

"Well?" Jordy blinked dumbly up at her. Didn't she know anything? Nobody ever got *well* from diabetes.

Nana licked her coral lipstick and looked away. "Better, I mean. You know. Under control."

Right. Control. Jordy let his eyelids drift closed. The infernal beeping echoed inside his head like a resident video game. "What *is* that?" he finally said aloud.

"What?"

"That beeping noise. It's driving me crazy."

"Oh, that." Nana cleared her throat. "It's from the heart monitor, see?"

Jordy touched his chest, felt the wire leads, the round patches stuck to his skin. A wave of panic rushed through him. What do I need a heart monitor for? I just had a little reaction, that's all. "Am I . . . I *am* okay, aren't I?" he stammered.

"For now," Nana said.

"What's that supposed to mean?"

"Just what I said. You're stable. For now. I guess the rest is up to you."

"What's this? Another lecture?"

Nana's eyes flashed. "We almost lost you, damn it! Don't you realize this is not a game here? This is your *life* we're talking about."

Jordy tried to turn away, but she cupped his chin and held it fast.

"You think you can run away from this, but you can't. It stinks, I know. And it's not fair. But the sooner you accept it, Jordy, the happier you're going to be."

"I-I wasn't trying to run away," Jordy said. "I was just . . ." Just what? Trying to show off for Cass? At least she was willing to admit *her* limitations. What was so shameful about him admitting his own? He curled his fingers around Nana's and held them tight. "Did I really almost . . . you know . . ." He fought with himself to say the word: *die.* If he didn't say it, then it couldn't happen, right?

"Let's just thank God for Cass," Nana said. "How

she made it up to you and back down again to call for help in time is beyond any of us. What I don't understand is why you were running away in the first place."

"We weren't," Jordy said, but the lie caught in his throat. Maybe Cass wasn't, but *he* was . . . and had been for the past eighteen months. Didn't he know that nobody ever ran away from diabetes? He'd been crazy to even try. Cass had known that all along, hadn't she? But he hadn't listened. "Please," he said, "let me see Cass."

Jordy watched the green blip of his heartbeat dance across the monitor as Nana went to fetch her. This wasn't TV; this was real. If the beeping stopped, so did he. Jordy shuddered at the thought and realized that there was no protest, no petition, no demonstration that could change *this* injustice. He, Jordan Michael Sondel, was a diabetic. And the sooner he stopped waging war against it, the sooner he'd find peace. Maybe sometimes it's better to surrender, he thought.

"Jordy? How you doing?" Cass tiptoed toward the bed, as if the sound of her footsteps would somehow make him feel worse. "I brought you something. Nothing big. But when I saw it downstairs at the gift shop, I knew it had your name on it. Here," she said. "Hold out your arm."

When he complied with the right one, tied to the

IV line, she rejected it in favor of his left. Then she buckled on a digital Timex. "It's just like you," she said. "Takes a licking and keeps on ticking."

Jordy's face went hot. He knew, of course, why she was giving it to him. She hadn't bought his little joke about watch-wearing being "against his religion" for a second. Now he'd have no excuse not to keep track of mealtimes and everything else he was supposed to. No excuse, that is, except for his own unwillingness. The truth is, Jordy thought, the buck stops here with me, myself. Not with Cass or Mom or Nana and Grandpa. It's my life, not theirs.

No matter how he figured it, it was high time to start making better choices. Diabetes had enough complications of its own. He didn't have to make matters worse by being out of control and giving fate the flying finger. His old, defensive spark of anger died unspoken and his voice cracked on a single word: "Thanks."

"Just use it, okay?" Cass winked, but the familiar light was gone from her eyes.

Jordy saw that she was chewing her lip. "Hey," he said, "I'm gonna be fine. Believe me. What is it? Mr. Cotter still giving you trouble? I figured that news reporter would have put him in his place by now."

"It's not that," Cass said. "It's Grandma. She wasn't in the car and Grandfather said I'd see her at the hospital, so naturally I thought—" She broke off, redfaced and upset. "But she's not here—anywhere. I even had one of the nurses check patient admissions when Grandfather went for some coffee."

"What does *he* say?"

"Nothing. Just that she's still downtown."

"That's it?"

"That, and 'first things first,' whatever that means. Nobody's telling me anything. I just hate it."

Jordy sighed. What did they have to do? *Demand* that their grandparents treat them like first-class citizens? He struggled through his memory to that morning, when he and Cass had set off for the Wind Caves. "I thought you said she was going for a checkup. Maybe she's still at the doctor's—downtown," he said. "Maybe you misunderstood."

"Maybe." Cass slapped a newspaper down on the bed. "Anyway, I thought you'd want to see this."

Jordy unfolded the Local section with one hand. The headline YOUTHS PROTEST TRAILER POLICY streamed across the top. His eyes watered as he tried to read the small, black print. At last he set it down, exhausted. "Just tell me. What's it all mean?"

Cass shrugged. "We're big heroes, I guess. And Mr. Cotter comes off like a real jerk. But it's funny, you know? All I care about right now is Grandma."

"I'm sure she's fine."

"*I'm* not," Cass said glumly. "But you can bet I'm going to find out."

"Atta girl!" Jordy crumpled his hand into a fist, saluting her weakly.

"Well . . ." Cass shrugged. "Guess I'll see you later, huh?"

Jordy nodded. "Give me forty-eight hours and I'll be rarin' to go."

Cass moved a step closer, flipped her hair off her shoulders. "I'm glad," she said. "Alta Mesa wouldn't be the same without you."

As she turned to go, a knot rose in Jordy's throat. He tried to blink away the sudden burning in his eyes. "Cass, wait!"

"You okay?"

He nodded, willed his heartbeat to return to normal. "What you did back there on the mountain—you saved my life, you know that?"

Cass avoided his gaze; he could see the color rise in her cheeks. "I-I guess I'm a lot stronger than I think, huh?"

Jordy reached for her hand, and she met him halfway, lacing her fingers in his. "Don't forget it," he said. "Promise?"

"I promise." She raised her eyes until they connected with his, and for a moment, he thought he could see her soul. "Jordy?"

"Yeah?"

"Even when I'm back in Iowa freezing my fanny off, I won't forget *you* either." Then she let go of his hand, averting her face and bolting for the door. It clicked open and hissed shut, and the hospital corridor swallowed her whole.

Jordy sighed, squeezing his lids over the watery blur. A headache tugged at the corners of his eyes, making him wince. Fingering the face of his new watch, he memorized the feel of its multifunction buttons. The beeping monitor droned on, and he smiled despite his pain. The sound was constant reassurance that he, like the watch, kept on ticking. Just as Cass had said.

Cass faced Grandfather, Hi, and Dottie as if they were members of a firing squad. No matter what they said, she was ready; she could take it. She didn't care if this *was* the waiting room, if other people *were* around. She had to know where Grandma was. Now. She'd waited two hours already. She'd been patient enough.

"Please," she said, "I'm not a dumb little kid. You don't need to protect me. Just tell me the truth."

Dottie patted Grandfather's hand, and Hi pressed his lips together, nodded his assent. "We'll be in Jordy's room, Ed," Dottie said. "You call us if there's anything—"

"Right," Hi chimed in. "Anything at all we can do, you just holler."

Grandfather slicked his hair back with his palms, accepted Dottie's hug stiffly in embarrassed silence. It was nothing personal, Cass realized now. Her grandfather just wasn't a hugger. At last he cleared his throat. "She's over at Phoenix General, honey. But it's only a precaution," he added quickly. "No need to worry, really. The doctor just wants to watch her. The stress of today and all."

Cass's mind raced. Was he blaming her and Jordy for whatever was wrong with Grandma? Grandfather was talking in circles. "I want to see her," she said.

Grandfather nodded. "We'll take a cab."

The taxi driver chattered on and on about upcoming Fiesta Bowl activities, preventing Cass from pumping Grandfather for more information. Not that he would say much anyway, she thought. Grandfather seemed to have his own schedule for answering her questions.

Fifteen minutes later he was guiding her by the elbow down Phoenix General's main corridor to the elevator. They got off on nine. As they passed the nurses' station, Cass noticed a large video screen with a stack of green-blip traces darting across it.

"Jordy had something like that," she said, more to reassure herself than to inform Grandfather. She looked up at him, saw the tight set of his jaw, and swallowed hard. "Did Grandma . . . did she have . . . a heart attack?"

Grandfather stopped abruptly and took her hands in his. "No. She didn't. Now, I don't want you to worry. She's going to come through this just fine," he said.

She searched the depths of his blue eyes for a flicker of dishonesty and was relieved not to find one. It was true then. Grandma was going to come through this. . . . Come through what? she wondered.

Grandfather eased open the door to T-986. There was only one bed in the cramped room. An accordian-style partition made up one wall. Grandma's eyes were closed. The covers over her chest moved upward in little jerks, then fell with the rush of her breath. Out the window in the distance, Cass could barely discern the mountain on which someone had emblazoned *Phoenix* and the arrow pointing west. Only this time, unlike that morning, she was way west of the arrow.

"Maybe we should go," Cass whispered. "So we don't wake her."

Grandfather shook his head and advanced to the bed. He pulled a chair closer and leaned forward in it, watching Grandma sleep. Cass hung back by the door, hugging herself, unable to suppress a sudden shiver. What's going on? Talk to me! Stop shutting me out!

Grandfather turned suddenly toward her, and she wondered whether she'd only thought the words or actually spoken them aloud. "Come sit a spell, Cassie," he said, more a plea than an order. "She . . ." He cleared his throat, began again. "I . . . we . . . need you. Lord, do we ever."

Cass's pulse quickened. She thought of that drive with Grandfather from the airport, how his reserve had put her on edge. She'd wanted instant love and acceptance; he'd pointed out that they were practically strangers. Now, unasked, he was offering what she'd always hoped for. All she had to do was take it. And yet . . .

"Why do you need me *now*?" she said, moving no closer than the end of the bed. "Why only now?"

Grandfather rubbed at his wedding-ring finger, avoiding her eyes. "Not *only* now," he said at last. "*Especially* now. There's a difference."

"Not to me." Though she tried to whisper, her voice cracked under the weight of her emotion.

Grandma's eyes fluttered open and lit softly on Cass. "Thank God," she murmured. "Ed said you were all right but I had to see for myself." She extended her hand and Cass stepped forward to take it. Grandma's squeeze seemed a halfhearted one.

"What's the matter with you?" Cass said. "Please, I want to know."

Her grandparents held a debate with their eyes. At last Grandma patted the bed, and Cass gingerly eased herself onto it. "Sweetie, it's my heart," Grandma said.

Cass eyed her grandfather reproachfully. "I thought you told me—"

"I said it wasn't a heart attack. And it *wasn't.*" Grandfather bristled, defending his earlier statement. "It's a blockage. Three, actually."

"We found out earlier this month, and they wanted to do a bypass. But I wouldn't let them."

"Why not?" I just found you and now we're out of time? Is that what you're going to tell me? Cass wished she could take hold of Grandma's shoulders and shake the whole story out of her—fast.

"I wouldn't let them, because I wanted to see *you* first. Not just see you but *know* you. Just in case . . . you know . . ." Grandma's voice trailed off and she dabbed at the corners of her eyes with the sheet.

So, that was the reason they had sent for her, and probably the explanation for her mother's saying yes. Words stuck in Cass's throat.

"We wanted to know our only grandchild," Grandfather said, "and we never did get to say good-bye to your father."

Small comfort I am, going off with Jordy the way I did, Cass thought. She struggled to breathe around the lump in her throat. "But why didn't Mom *tell* me about the bypass? Why was it all such a big secret?"

"Leah didn't want your pity, honey. Wouldn't see you any other way. Your mama gave us her word that you'd come with an open mind. And we're grateful you did."

Grandma patted a radio-shaped box that protruded from a breast pocket in her hospital gown. "Those nurses must be getting quite an eyeful," she said. "My heart's doing a jig, I'll tell you that. I've been so worried that you'd be angry when you knew the truth."

"Angry?" The word flew from her mouth, seemed to press Grandma deeper into her pillow. "Why would I be angry?"

"All those years you never heard from us," Grandma said. "You must have thought we didn't care."

Cass pictured the stack of letters and cards that Jordy had shown her. "It's not *your* fault what I thought," she said. "It's Mom's."

Grandma licked her lips, eased a gray wisp back from her forehead. "I'm not saying it was and I'm not saying it wasn't," she said, reaching for Grandfather's hand.

"It's okay," Cass said. "Jordy showed me the letters. I know Mom sent them back."

"She loves you so much," Grandma said, her eyes shiny with tears. "Who can blame her? I know she was just afraid of losing you, too, as well as your dad."

"How could she lose me?" Cass couldn't believe Grandma was lying there defending *Mom* of all people. Incredible.

Grandfather cleared his throat, drew his lips from side to side. "I think maybe I can explain," he said. "You see, after Peter died on that blasted motorcycle, we blamed your mother. Oh, she was a wild little thing back then, and we never really accepted her. Not really. You've got to understand we were crazy with grief. Otherwise we'd never have said . . . never have done what . . ."

Grandfather broke off and blew his nose loudly into a crisp white handkerchief. Cass could see him fighting with himself to go on, but he was losing the battle. She struggled to finish his thought. What could they have said in their grief that would have made Mom so afraid of losing her?

"You threatened to take me away from her, didn't you?" Cass said gently. An ironic smile creased her cheeks. Mom was great as far as she went, but even she would admit that Cass had practically raised herself. And now, there was no threat;

the McFerrens were old and sick, and her mother knew it was safe to let her come. "That's why she kept us apart, isn't it?"

Grandma and Grandfather nodded in unison. "But we'd never have done it," Grandma added quickly.

Cass let slip a giggle. "Maybe you should have," she said. "Maybe you'd have done me a favor."

"Now, now." Grandfather wagged a finger. "Kelly's done all right raising you."

"Whatever," Cass said. There was no sense telling them stuff they were powerless to change. "The main thing now is to get you well."

Grandma nodded. "Dr. Ruiz wants to do the bypass the day after tomorrow. What's that? The thirtieth?"

"I-I think so," Cass said. And Jordy's leaving on the first, she remembered.

"You're flying home on the sixth?"

"Uh-huh." That was the plan anyway, but who knew what the trailer-park manager had in mind. Maybe the newspaper article had mellowed him; then again, maybe it had only ticked him off. Cass tried to imagine Mr. Cotter evicting her grandparents with Grandma fresh out of bypass surgery. What would the newspapers say about a thing like that? She'd have to ask Jordy the name of that reporter, just in case.

"Cassie?" Grandma snapped her fingers. "Darling, I was asking if you'd mind Muffin for me."

Cass grinned. "Of course. And don't worry. I'll make sure she goes three times before I bring her inside."

"And Monday night," Grandma said, "maybe you'll play a card or two for me at bingo. Make that three."

"Three it is. You just relax and let me take care of everything. I'll have Grandpa all fattened up by the time you're back on your feet. Like I told you before, I'm a good cook." Cass leaned toward her grandmother until their noses met and touched.

"Between you and me," Grandma whispered, "he *is* a little skinny, isn't he?"

Cass nodded, suppressing a giggle. Then she hugged Grandma long and close, as if she could transfuse her own sudden strength into her grandmother's body. The older woman's skin smelled of alcohol and baby powder, and the reality that Cass might never again hug this loving, eccentric woman made a sob catch in her chest.

"You're a lot stronger than you know," she whispered. "Don't you forget that. Promise?"

When Grandma nodded, Cass hugged her again. And again, because threes were lucky.

Sheri Cooper Sinykin

was born in Chicago, Illinois, the eldest of four children, and grew up in Sacramento, California. She earned a bachelor's degree in communications-journalism from Stanford University, worked for a brief time as a news reporter, and wrote feature stories for a hospital magazine.

As a child, Sheri enjoyed writing, swimming, ballet, and summer camp. She has traveled to Hawaii and Europe, as well as Central and South America. She collects dolls from all over the world, and says she is more frustrated than successful at windsurfing but enjoys trying. She has published several middle-grade and young-adult novels. Sheri and her husband, a lawyer and land developer, and three sons live in Madison, Wisconsin.